Edgar Allan Poe (1809–1849) is America's favorite writer of mystery and terror. Nothing is more indicative of Poe's genius than his increasing popularity 150 years after his death.

Throughout his brief, yet troubled, life, Poe wrote over 140 published poems and stories. He was already a published author and magazine editor when he achieved national fame for "The Raven" in 1845. This poem was reprinted constantly in newspapers, becoming his most widely read piece and making him the master of the macabre in America. Eventually, Poe's fame would spread through the world.

The French, in particular, were so impressed with his use of imagery that they used his poetry as a guide for their own. In addition, Poe has been called the father of the modern short story and the inventor of detective fiction. Today's mystery stories can be traced back over a century to Poe's "Murders in the Rue Morgue," the first detective story and perhaps the model for all others.

Forgotten Tales by Edgar Allan Poe celebrates several overlooked stories — stories that scare and tease and surprise, but that simply aren't as well known as the others. Here is a reminder that there is more of Poe for us to read, to enjoy . . . and to fear.

EDGAR ALLAN POE

FORGOTTEN TALES

SCHOLASTIC INC.
New York Toronto London Auckland Sydney

ISBN 0-590-76371-7

12 11 10 9 8 7 6 5 4 3 2 1   7 8 9/9 0 1 2/0

Printed in the U.S.A.
First Scholastic printing, October 1997

CONTENTS

Printed in the USA

First Scholastic printing, October 1997

THE SPECTACLES

Many years ago, it was the fashion to ridicule the idea of "love at first sight"; but those who think, not less than those who feel deeply, have always advocated its existence. Modern discoveries, indeed, in what may be termed ethical magnetism or magneto-æsthetics, render it probable that the most natural, and, consequently, the truest and most intense of the human affections are those which arise in the heart as if by electric sympathy — in a word, that the brightest and most enduring of the psychal fetters are those which are riveted by a glance. The confession I am about to make will add another to the already almost innumerable instances of the truth of the position.

My story requires that I should be somewhat minute. I am still a very young man — not yet twenty-two years of age. My name, at present, is a very usual and rather plebeian one — Simpson. I say "at present"; for it is only lately that I have been so called — having legislatively adopted this surname within the last year, in order to receive a large inheritance left me by a distant male relative, Adolphus Simpson, Esq. The bequest was conditioned upon my taking the name of the testator — the family, not the Christian name; my Christian name is Napoleon Bonaparte — or, more properly, these are my first and middle appellations.

I assumed the name, Simpson, with some reluctance, as in my true patronym, Froissart, I felt a very pardonable pride — believing that I could trace a descent from the immortal author of the "Chronicles." While on the subject of names, by the by, I may mention a singular coincidence of sound attending the names of some of my immediate predecessors. My father was a Monsieur Froissart, of Paris. His wife — my mother, whom he married at fifteen — was a Mademoiselle Croissart, eldest daughter of Croissart the banker; whose wife, again, being only sixteen when married, was the eldest daughter of one Victor Voissart. Monsieur Voissart, very singularly, had married a lady of similar name — a Mademoiselle Moissart. She, too, was quite a child when married; and her mother, also, Madame Moissart, was only fourteen when led to the altar. These early marriages are usual in France. Here, however, are Moissart, Voissart, Croissart, and Froissart, all in the direct line of descent. My own name, though, as I say, became Simpson, by act of Legislature, and with so much repugnance on my part, that, at one period, I actually hesitated about accepting the legacy with the useless and annoying *proviso* attached.

As to personal endowments, I am by no means deficient. On the contrary, I believe that I am well made, and possess what nine tenths of the world would call a handsome face. In height I am five feet eleven. My hair is black and curling. My nose is sufficiently good. My eyes are large and gray; although, in fact, they are weak to a very inconvenient degree, still no defect in this regard would be suspected from their appearance. The weakness itself, however, has always much annoyed me, and I have resorted to every remedy — short of wearing glasses. Being youthful and good-looking,

I naturally dislike these, and have resolutely refused to employ them. I know nothing, indeed, which so disfigures the countenance of a young person, or so impresses every feature with an air of demureness, if not altogether of sanctimoniousness and of age. An eye-glass, on the other hand, has a savor of downright foppery and affectation. I have hitherto managed as well as I could without either. But something too much of these merely personal details, which, after all, are of little importance. I will content myself with saying, in addition, that my temperament is sanguine, rash, ardent, enthusiastic — and that all my life I have been a devoted admirer of the women.

One night last winter I entered a box at the P—— Theatre, in company with a friend, Mr. Talbot. It was an opera night, and the bills presented a very rare attraction, so that the house was excessively crowded. We were in time, however, to obtain the front seats which had been reserved for us, and into which, with some little difficulty, we elbowed our way.

For two hours my companion, who was a musical *fanatico*, gave his undivided attention to the stage; and, in the meantime, I amused myself by observing the audience, which consisted, in chief part, of the very *élite* of the city. Having satisfied myself upon this point, I was about turning my eyes to the *prima donna*, when they were arrested and riveted by a figure in one of the private boxes which had escaped my observation.

If I live a thousand years I can never forget the intense emotion with which I regarded this figure. It was that of a female, the most exquisite I had ever beheld. The face was so far turned toward the stage that, for some minutes, I could not obtain a view of it, — but the form was *divine*;

no other words can sufficiently express its magnficent proportion, — and even the term "divine" seems ridiculously
feeble as I write it.

The magic of a lovely form in woman — the necro-
mancy of female gracefulness — was always a power which
I had found it impossible to resist; but here was grace per-
sonified, incarnate, the *beau idéal* of my wildest and most
enthusiastic visions. The figure, almost all of which the construction of the box permitted to be seen, was somewhat
above the medium height, and nearly approached, without
positively reaching, the majestic. Its perfect fulness and
tournure were delicious. The head, of which only the back
was visible, rivalled in outline that of the Greek Psyche, and
was rather displayed than concealed by an elegant cap of
gaze aérienne, which put me in mind of the *ventum textilem*
of Apuleius. The right arm hung over the balustrade of the
box, and thrilled every nerve of my frame with its exquisite
symmetry. Its upper portion was draperied by one of the
loose open sleeves now in fashion. This extended but little
below the elbow. Beneath it was worn an under one of some
frail material, close-fitting, and terminated by a cuff of rich
lace, which fell gracefully over the top of the hand, reveal-
ing only the delicate fingers, upon one of which sparkled a
diamond ring, which I at once saw was of extraordinary
value. The admirable roundness of the wrist was well set off
by a bracelet which encircled it, and which also was orna-
mented and clasped by a magnificent *aigrette* of jewels, —
telling, in words that could not be mistaken, at once of the
wealth and fastidious taste of the wearer.

I gazed at this queenly apparition for at least half an
hour, as if I had been suddenly converted to stone; and,
during this period, I felt the full force and truth of all that

has been said or sung concerning "love at first sight." My feelings were totally different from any which I had hitherto experienced, in the presence of even the most celebrated specimens of female loveliness. An unaccountable, and what I am compelled to consider a *magnetic*, sympathy of soul for soul, seemed to rivet, not only my vision, but my whole powers of thought and feeling, upon the admirable object before me. I saw — I felt — I knew that I was deeply, madly, irrevocably in love — and this even before seeing the face of the person beloved. So intense, indeed, was the passion that consumed me, that I really believe it would have received little if any abatement had the features, yet unseen, proved of merely ordinary character; so anomalous is the nature of the only true love — of the love at first sight — and so little really dependent is it upon the external conditions which only seem to create and control it.

While I was thus wrapped in admiration of this lovely vision, a sudden disturbance among the audience caused her to turn her head partially toward me, so that I beheld the entire profile of the face. Its beauty even exceeded my anticipations — and yet there was something about it which disappointed me without my being able to tell exactly what it was. I said "disappointed," but this is not altogether the word. My sentiments were at once quieted and exalted. They partook less of transport and more of calm enthusiasm — of enthusiastic repose. This state of feeling arose, perhaps, from the Madonna-like and matronly air of the face; and yet I at once understood that it could not have arisen entirely from this. There was something else — some mystery which I could not develop — some expression about the countenance which slightly disturbed me while it greatly heightened my interest. In fact, I was just in that condition of mind which prepares a young and susceptible man for any act of extravagance. Had the lady been alone, I should undoubtedly have entered her box and accosted her at all hazards; but, fortunately, she was attended by two companions — a gentleman, and a strikingly beautiful woman, to all appearance a few years younger than herself.

I revolved in my mind a thousand schemes by which I might obtain, hereafter, an introduction to the elder lady, or, for the present, at all events, a more distinct view of her beauty. I would have removed my position to one nearer her own, but the crowded state of the theatre rendered this impossible; and the stern decrees of Fashion had, of late, imperatively prohibited the use of the opera-glass, in a case such as this, even had I been so fortunate as to have one with me — but I had not — and was thus in despair.

At length I bethought me of applying to my companion.

"Talbot," I said, "*you* have an opera-glass. Let me have it."

"An opera-glass! — no! — what do you suppose *I* would be doing with an opera-glass?" Here he turned impatiently toward the stage.

"But, Talbot," I continued, pulling him by the shoulder, "listen to me, will you? Do you see the stage-box? — there! — no, the next. — Did you ever behold as lovely a woman?"

"She is very beautiful, no doubt," he said.

"I wonder who she can be?"

"Why, in the name of all that is angelic, don't you *know* who she is? 'Not to know her argues yourself unknown.' She is the celebrated Madame Lalande — the beauty of the day *par excellence*, and the talk of the whole town. Im-

mensely wealthy too — a widow — and a great match —
has just arrived from Paris."

"Do you know her?"

"Yes — I have the honor."

"Will you introduce me?"

"Assuredly — with the greatest pleasure; when shall it
be?"

"To-morrow, at one, I will call upon you at B——'s."

"Very good; and now *do* hold your tongue, *if* you can."

In this latter respect I was forced to take Talbot's advice;
for he remained obstinately deaf to every further question
or suggestion, and occupied himself exclusively for the rest
of the evening with what was transacting upon the stage.

In the meantime I kept my eyes riveted on Madame Lalande, and at length had the good fortune to obtain a full
front view of her face. It was exquisitely lovely: this, of
course, my heart had told me before, even had not Talbot
fully satisfied me upon the point — but still the unintelligible something disturbed me. I finally concluded that my
senses were impressed by a certain air of gravity, sadness, or,
still more properly, of weariness, which took something
from the youth and freshness of the countenance, only to
endow it with a seraphic tenderness and majesty, and thus,
of course, to my enthusiastic and romantic temperament,
with an interest tenfold.

While I thus feasted my eyes, I perceived, at last, to my
great trepidation, by an almost imperceptible start on the
part of the lady, that she had become suddenly aware of the
intensity of my gaze. Still, I was absolutely fascinated, and
could not withdraw it, even for an instant. She turned aside
her face, and again I saw only the chiselled contour of the

back portion of the head. After some minutes, as if urged
by curiosity to see if I was still looking, she gradually
brought her face again around and again encountered my
burning gaze. Her large dark eyes fell instantly, and a deep
blush mantled her cheek. But what was my astonishment at
perceiving that she not only did not a second time avert her
head, but that she actually took from her girdle a double
eye-glass — elevated it — adjusted it — and then regarded
me through it, intently and deliberately, for the space of
several minutes.

Had a thunderbolt fallen at my feet I could not have
been more thoroughly astounded — astounded *only* — not
offended or disgusted in the slightest degree; although an
action so bold in any other woman would have been likely
to offend or disgust. But the whole thing was done with so
much quietude — so much *nonchalance* — so much repose
— with so evident an air of the highest breeding, in short
— that nothing of mere effrontery was perceptible, and my
sole sentiments were those of admiration and surprise.

I observed that, upon her first elevation of the glass, she
had seemed satisfied with a momentary inspection of my
person, and was withdrawing the instrument, when, as if
struck by a second thought, she resumed it, and so continued to regard me with fixed attention for the space of several minutes — for five minutes, at the very least, I am sure.

This action, so remarkable in an American theatre, attracted very general observation, and gave rise to an indefinite movement, or *buzz*, among the audience, which for a
moment filled me with confusion, but produced no visible
effect upon the countenance of Madame Lalande.

Having satisfied her curiosity — if such it was — she
dropped the glass, and quietly gave her attention again to

the stage; her profile now being turned toward myself, as before. I continued to watch her unremittingly, although I was fully conscious of my rudeness in so doing. Presently I saw the head slowly and slightly change its position; and soon I became convinced that the lady, while pretending to look at the stage was, in fact, attentively regarding myself. It is needless to say what effect this conduct, on the part of so fascinating a woman, had upon my excitable mind.

Having thus scrutinized me for perhaps a quarter of an hour, the fair object of my passion addressed the gentleman who attended her, and, while she spoke, I saw distinctly, by the glances of both, that the conversation had reference to myself.

Upon its conclusion, Madame Lalande again turned toward the stage, and, for a few minutes, seemed absorbed in the performances. At the expiration of this period, however, I was thrown into an extremity of agitation by seeing her unfold, for the second time, the eye-glass which hung at her side, fully confront me as before, and, disregarding the renewed buzz of the audience, survey me, from head to foot, with the same miraculous composure which had previously so delighted and confounded my soul.

This extraordinary behavior, by throwing me into a perfect fever of excitement — into an absolute delirium of love — served rather to embolden than to disconcert me. In the mad intensity of my devotion, I forgot every thing but the presence and the majestic loveliness of the vision which confronted my gaze. Watching my opportunity, when I thought the audience were fully engaged with the opera, I at length caught the eyes of Madame Lalande, and, upon the instant, made a slight but unmistakable bow.

She blushed very deeply — then averted her eyes —

then slowly and cautiously looked around, apparently to see if my rash action had been noticed — then leaned over toward the gentleman who sat by her side.

I now felt a burning sense of the impropriety I had committed, and expected nothing less than instant exposure; while a vision of pistols upon the morrow floated rapidly and uncomfortably through my brain. I was greatly and immediately relieved, however, when I saw the lady merely hand the gentleman a play-bill, without speaking; but the reader may form some feeble conception of my astonishment — of my *profound* amazement — my delirious bewilderment of heart and soul — when, instantly afterward, having again glanced furtively around, she allowed her bright eyes to set fully and steadily upon my own, and then, with a faint smile, disclosing a bright line of her pearly teeth, made two dinstinct, pointed, and unequivocal affirmative inclinations of the head.

It is useless, of course, to dwell upon my joy — upon my transport — upon my illimitable ecstasy of heart. If ever man was mad with excess of happiness, it was myself at that moment. I loved. This was my *first* love — so I felt it to be. It was love supreme — indescribable. It was "love at first sight"; and at first sight, too, it had been appreciated and *returned.*

Yes, returned. How and why should I doubt it for an instant. What other construction could I possibly put upon such conduct, on the part of a lady so beautiful — so wealthy — evidently so accomplished — of so high breeding — of so lofty a position in society — in every regard so entirely respectable as I felt assured was Madame Lalande? Yes, she loved me — she returned the enthusiasm of my love, with an enthusiasm as blind — as uncompromising

— as uncalculating — as abandoned — and as utterly un-bounded as my own! These delicious fancies and reflec-tions, however, were now interrupted by the falling of the drop-curtain. The audience arose; and the usual tumult im-mediately supervened. Quitting Talbot abruptly, I made every effort to force my way into closer proximity with Madame Lalande. Having failed in this, on account of the crowd, I at length gave up the chase, and bent my steps homeward; consoling myself for my disappointment in not having been able to touch even the hem of her robe, by the reflection that I should be introduced by Talbot, in due form, upon the morrow.

This morrow at last came; that is to say, a day finally dawned upon a long and weary night of impatience; and then the hours until "one" were snail-paced, dreary, and in-numerable. But even Stamboul, it is said, shall have an end, and there came an end to this long delay. The clock struck. As the last echo ceased, I stepped into B——'s and inquired for Talbot.

"Out," said the footman — Talbot's own.

"Out!" I replied, staggering back half a dozen paces — "let me tell you, my fine fellow, that this thing is thoroughly impossible and impracticable; Mr. Talbot is *not* out. What do you mean?"

"Nothing, sir; only Mr. Talbot is not in. That's all. He rode over to S——, immediately after breakfast, and left word that he would not be in town again for a week."

I stood petrified with horror and rage. I endeavored to reply, but my tongue refused its office. At length I turned on my heel, livid with wrath, and inwardly consigning the whole tribe of the Talbots to the innermost regions of Ere-bus. It was evident that my considerate friend, *il fanatico*, had quite forgotten his appointment with myself — had forgotten it as soon as it was made. At no time was he a very scrupulous man of his word. There was no help for it; so smothering my vexation as well as I could, I strolled moodily up the street, propounding futile inquiries about Madame Lalande to every male acquaintance I met. By report she was known, I found, to all — to many by sight — but she had been in town only a few weeks, and there were very few, therefore, who claimed her personal acquaintance. These few, being still comparatively strangers, could not, or would not, take the liberty of introducing me through the formality of a morning call. While I stood thus, in despair, conversing with a trio of friends upon the all-absorbing subject of my heart, it so happened that the subject itself passed by.

"As I live, there she is!" cried one.

"Surprisingly beautiful!" exclaimed a second.

"An angel upon earth!" ejaculated a third.

I looked; and in an open carriage which approached us, passing slowly down the street, sat the enchanting vision of the opera, accompanied by the younger lady who had occupied a portion of her box.

"Her companion also wears remarkably well," said the one of my trio who had spoken first.

"Astonishingly," said the second; "still quite a brilliant air; but art will do wonders. Upon my word, she looks better than she did at Paris five years ago. A beautiful woman still; — don't you think so, Froissart? — Simpson, I mean."

"*Still!*" said I, "and why shouldn't she be? But compared with her friend she is as a rushlight to the evening star — a glow-worm to Antares."

"Ha! ha! ha! — why, Simpson, you have an astonishing

tact at making discoveries — original ones, I mean." And here we separated, while one of the trio began humming a gay *vaudeville*, of which I caught only the lines —

> Ninon, Ninon, Ninon à bas —
> A bas Ninon de L'Enclos!

During this little scene, however, one thing had served greatly to console me, although it fed the passion by which I was consumed. As the carriage of Madame Lalande rolled by our group, I had observed that she recognized me; and more than this, she had blessed me, by the most seraphic of all imaginable smiles, with no equivocal mark of the recognition.

As for an introduction, I was obliged to abandon all hope of it, until such time as Talbot should think proper to return from the country. In the meantime I perseveringly frequented every reputable place of public amusement; and, at length, at the theatre, where I first saw her, I had the supreme bliss of meeting her, and of exchanging glances with her once again. This did not occur, however, until the lapse of a fortnight. Every day, in the *interim*, I had inquired for Talbot at his hotel, and every day had been thrown into a spasm of wrath by the everlasting "Not come home yet" of his footman.

Upon the evening in question, therefore, I was in a condition little short of madness. Madame Lalande, I had been told, was a Parisian — had lately arrived from Paris — might she not suddenly return? — return before Talbot came back — and might she not be thus lost to me forever? The thought was too terrible to bear. Since my future happiness was at issue, I resolved to act with a manly decision.

In a word, upon the breaking up of the play, I traced the lady to her residence, noted the address, and the next morning sent her a full and elaborate letter, in which I poured out my whole heart.

I spoke boldly, freely — in a word, I spoke with passion. I concealed nothing — nothing even of my weakness. I alluded to the romantic circumstances of our first meeting — even to the glances which had passed between us. I went so far as to say that I felt assured of her love; while I offered this assurance, and my own intensity of devotion, as two excuses for my otherwise unpardonable conduct. As a third, I spoke of my fear that she might quit the city before I could have the opportunity of a formal introduction. I concluded the most wildly enthusiastic epistle ever penned, with a frank declaration of my worldly circumstances — of my affluence — and with an offer of my heart and of my hand.

In an agony of expectation I awaited the reply. After what seemed the lapse of a century it came.

Yes, *actually came*. Romantic as all this may appear, I really received a letter from Madame Lalande — the beautiful, the wealthy, the idolized Madame Lalande. Her eyes — her magnificient eyes, had not belied her noble heart. Like a true Frenchwoman, as she was, she had obeyed the frank dictates of her reason — the generous impulses of her nature — despising the conventional pruderies of the world. She had *not* scorned my proposals. She had *not* sheltered herself in silence. She had *not* returned my letter unopened. She had even sent me, in reply, one penned by her own exquisite fingers. It ran thus:

"Monsieur Simpson vill pardonne me for not compose de butefulle tong of his contrée so vell as might. It is only

de late dat I am arrive, and not yet ave de opportunité for
to — l'étudier.

"Vid dis apologie for the manière, I vill now say dat,
hélas! — Monsieur Simpson ave guess but de too true.
Need I say de more? Hélas! am I not ready speak de too
moshe?

"EUGÉNIE LALANDE"

This noble-spirited note I kissed a million times, and
committed, no doubt, on its account, a thousand other extravagances that have now escaped my memory. Still Talbot
would not return. Alas! could he have formed even the
vaguest idea of the suffering his absence had occasioned his
friend, would not his sympathizing nature have flown immediately to my relief? Still, however, he came *not*. I wrote.
He replied. He was detained by urgent business — but
would shortly return. He begged me not to be impatient —
to moderate my transports — to read soothing books — to
drink nothing stronger than Hock — and to bring the con-
solations of philosophy to my aid. The fool! if he could not
come himself, why, in the name of every thing rational,
could he not have enclosed me a letter of presentation? I
wrote him again, entreating him to forward one forthwith.
My letter was returned by *that* footman, with the following
endorsement in pencil. The scoundrel had joined his master in the country:

"Left S—— yesterday, for parts unknown — did not say
where — or when be back — so thought best to return letter, knowing your handwriting, and as how you is always,
more or less, in a hurry.

"Yours sincerely,   STUBBS"

After this, it is needless to say, that I devoted to the infernal deities both master and valet: — but there was little use in anger, and no consolation at all in complaint.

But I had yet a resource left, in my constitutional audacity. Hitherto it had served me well, and I now resolved to make it avail me to the end. Besides, after the correspondence which had passed between us, what act of mere informality *could* I commit, within bounds, that ought to be regarded as indecorous by Madame Lalande? Since the affair of the letter, I had been in the habit of watching her house, and thus discovered that, about twilight, it was her custom to promenade, attended only by a negro in livery, in a public square overlooked by her windows. Here, amid the luxuriant and shadowing groves, in the gray gloom of a sweet midsummer evening, I observed my opportunity and accosted her.

The better to deceive the servant in attendance, I did this with the assured air of an old and familiar acquaintance. With a presence of mind truly Parisian, she took the cue at once, and, to greet me, held out the most bewitchingly little of hands. The valet at once fell into the rear; and now, with hearts full to overflowing, we discoursed long and unreservedly of our love.

As Madame Lalande spoke English even less fluently than she wrote it, our conversation was necessarily in French. In this sweet tongue, so adapted to passion, I gave loose to the impetuous enthusiasm of my nature, and, with all the eloquence I could command, besought her to consent to an immediate marriage.

At this impatience she smiled. She urged the old story of decorum — that bug-bear which deters so many from bliss until the opportunity for bliss has forever gone by. I had most imprudently made it known among my friends, she observed, that I desired her acquaintance — thus that I did not possess it — thus, again, there was no possibility of concealing the date of our first knowledge of each other. And then she adverted, with a blush, to the extreme recency of this date. To wed immediately would be improper — would be indecorous — would be *outré*. All this she said with a charming air of *naïveté* which enraptured while it grieved and convinced me. She went even so far as to accuse me, laughingly, of rashness — of imprudence. She bade me remember that I really even knew not who she was — what were her prospects, her connections, her standing in society. She begged me, but with a sigh, to reconsider my proposal, and termed my love an infatuation — a will o' the wisp — a fancy or fantasy of the moment — a baseless and unstable creation rather of the imagination than of the heart. These things she uttered as the shadows of the sweet twilight, gathered darkly and more darkly around us — and then, with a gentle pressure of her fairy-like hand, overthrew, in a single sweet instant, all the argumentative fabric she had reared.

I replied as best I could — as only a true lover can. I spoke at length, and perseveringly of my devotion, of my passion — of her exceeding beauty, and of my own enthusiastic admiration. In conclusion, I dwelt, with a convincing energy, upon the perils that encompass the course of love — that course of true love that never did run smooth, — and thus deduced the manifest danger of rendering that course unnecessarily long.

This latter argument seemed finally to soften the rigor of her determination. She relented; but there was yet an obstacle, she said, which she felt assured I had not properly

considered. This was a delicate point — for a woman to
urge, especially so; in mentioning it, she saw that she must
make a sacrifice of her feelings; still, for *me*, every sacrifice
should be made. She alluded to the topic of *age*. Was I
aware — was I fully aware of the discrepancy between us?
That the age of the husband should surpass by a few years
— even by fifteen or twenty — the age of the wife, was regarded by the world as admissible, and, indeed, as even
proper; but she had always entertained the belief that the
years of the wife should *never* exceed in number those of the
husband. A discrepancy of this unnatural kind gave rise, too
frequently, alas! to a life of unhappiness. Now she was aware
that my own age did not exceed two and twenty; and I, on
the contrary, perhaps, was *not* aware that the years of my
Eugénie extended very considerably beyond that sum.

About all this there was a nobility of soul — a dignity of
candor — which   delighted — which   enchanted   me —
which eternally riveted my chains. I could scarcely restrain
the excessive transport which possessed me.

"My sweetest Eugénie," I cried, "what is all this about
which you are discoursing? Your years surpass in some measure my own. But what then? The customs of the world are
so many conventional follies. To those who love as ourselves, in what respect differs a year from an hour? I am
twenty-two, you say; granted: indeed, you may as well call
me, at once, twenty-three. Now you yourself, my dearest
Eugénie, can have numbered no more than — can have
numbered no more than — no more than — than — than
— than — "

Here I paused for an instant, in the expectation that
Madame Lalande would interrupt me by supplying her true
age. But a Frenchwoman is seldom direct, and has always,

by way of answer to an embarrassing query, some little practical reply of her own. In the present instance, Eugénie, who for a few moments past had seemed to be searching for something in her bosom, at length let fall upon the glass a miniature, which I immediately picked up and presented to her.

"Keep it!" she said, with one of her most ravishing smiles. "Keep it for my sake — for the sake of her whom it too flatteringly represents. Besides, upon the back of the trinket you may discover, perhaps, the very information you seem to desire. It is now, to be sure, growing rather dark — but you can examine it at your leisure in the morning. In the meantime, you shall be my escort home to-night. My friends are about holding a little musical *levée*. I can promise you, too, some good singing. We French are not nearly so punctilious as you Americans, and I shall have no difficulty in smuggling you in, in the character of an old acquaintance."

With this, she took my arm, and I attended her home. The mansion was quite a fine one, and, I believe, furnished in good taste. Of this latter point, however, I am scarcely qualified to judge; for it was just dark as we arrived; and in American mansions of the better sort lights seldom, during the heat of the summer, make their appearance at this, the most pleasant period of the day. In about an hour after my arrival, to be sure, a single shaded solar lamp was lit in the principal drawing-room; and this apartment, I could thus see, was arranged with unusual good taste and even splendor; but two other rooms of the suite, and in which the company chiefly assembled, remained, during the whole evening, in a very agreeable shadow. This is a well-conceived custom, giving the party at least a choice of light

or shade, and one which our friends over the water could
not do better than immediately adopt.

The evening thus spent was unquestionably the most delicious of my life. Madame Lalande had not overrated the
musical abilities of her friends; and the singing I here heard
I had never heard excelled in any private circle out of
Vienna. The instrumental performers were many and of
superior talents. The vocalists were chiefly ladies, and no individual sang less than well. At length, upon a peremptory
call for "Madame Lalande," she arose at once, without affectation or demur, from the *chaise longue* upon which she
had sat by my side, and, accompanied by one or two gentlemen and her female friend of the opera, repaired to the
piano in the main drawing-room. I would have escorted her
myself, but felt that, under the circumstances of my introduction to the house, I had better remain unobserved
where I was. I was thus deprived of the pleasure of seeing,
although not of hearing, her sing.

The impression she produced upon the company seemed
electrical — but the effect upon myself was something even
more. I know not how adequately to describe it. It arose in
part, no doubt, from the sentiment of love with which I
was imbued; but chiefly from my conviction of the extreme
sensibility of the singer. It is beyond the reach of art to endow either air or recitative with more impassioned *expression* than was hers. Her utterance of the romance in Otello
— the tone with which she gave the words *"Sul mio sasso,"*
in the Capuletti — is ringing in my memory yet. Her lower
tones were absolutely miraculous. Her voice embraced three
complete octaves, extending from the contralto D to the D
upper soprano, and, though sufficiently powerful to have
filled the San Carlos, executed, with the minutest precision,

every difficulty of vocal composition — ascending and descending scales, cadences, or *fioriture*. In the finale of the Sonnambula, she brought about a most remarkable effect at the words:

> Ah! non giunge uman pensiero
> Al contento ond 'io son piena.

Here, in imitation of Malibran, she modified the original phrase of Bellini, so as to let her voice descend to the tenor G, when, by a rapid transition, she struck the G above the treble stave, springing over an interval of two octaves.

Upon rising from the piano after these miracles of vocal execution, she resumed her seat by my side; when I expressed to her, in terms of the deepest enthusiasm, my delight at her performance. Of my surprise I said nothing, and yet was I most unfeignedly surprised; for a certain feebleness, or rather a certain tremulous indecision of voice in ordinary conversation, had prepared me to anticipate that, in singing, she would not acquit herself with any remarkable ability.

Our conversation was now long, earnest, uninterrupted, and totally unreserved. She made me relate many of the earlier passages of my life, and listened with breathless attention to every word of the narrative. I concealed nothing — felt that I had a right to conceal nothing — from her confiding affection. Encouraged by her candor upon the delicate point of her age, I entered, with perfect frankness, not only into a detail of my many minor vices, but made full confession of those moral and even of those physical infirmities, the disclosure of which, in demanding so much higher a degree of courage, is so much surer an evidence of

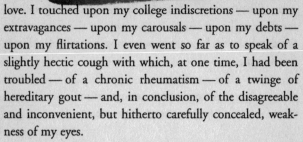

love. I touched upon my college indiscretions — upon my extravagances — upon my carousals — upon my debts — upon my flirtations. I even went so far as to speak of a slightly hectic cough with which, at one time, I had been troubled — of a chronic rheumatism — of a twinge of hereditary gout — and, in conclusion, of the disagreeable and inconvenient, but hitherto carefully concealed, weakness of my eyes.

"Upon this latter point," said Madame Lalande, laughingly, "you have been surely injudicious in coming to confession; for, without the confession, I take it for granted that no one would have accused you of the crime. By the by," she continued, "have you any recollection — " and here I fancied that a blush, even through the gloom of the apartment, became distinctly visible upon her cheek — "have you any recollection, *mon cher ami* of this little ocular assistant which now depends from my neck?"

As she spoke she twirled in her fingers the identical double eye-glass, which had so overwhelmed me with confusion at the opera.

"Full well — alas! do I remember it," I exclaimed, pressing passionately the delicate hand which offered the glasses for my inspection. They formed a complex and magnificent toy, richly chased and filigreed, and gleaming with jewels which, even in the deficient light, I could not help perceiving were of high value.

"*Eh bien! mon ami,*" she resumed with a certain *empressement* of manner that rather surprised me — "*Eh bien! mon ami*, you have earnestly besought of me a favor which you have been pleased to denominate priceless. You have demanded of me my hand upon the morrow. Should I yield to your entreaties — and, I may add, to the pleadings of my own bosom — would I not be entitled to demand of you a very — a very little boon in return?"

"Name it!" I exclaimed with an energy that had nearly drawn upon us the observation of the company, and restrained by their presence alone from throwing myself impetuously at her feet. "Name it, my beloved, my Eugénie, my own! — name it! — but, alas! it is already yielded ere named."

"You shall conquer, then, *mon ami*," said she, "for the sake of the Eugénie whom you love, this little weakness which you have at last confessed — this weakness more moral than physical — and which, let me assure you, is so unbecoming the nobility of your real nature — so inconsistent with the candor of your usual character — and which, if permitted further control, will assuredly involve you, sooner or later, in some very disagreeable scrape. You shall conquer, for my sake, this affectation which leads you, as you yourself acknowledge, to the tacit or implied denial of your infirmity of vision. For, this infirmity you virtually deny, in refusing to employ the customary means for its relief. You will understand me to say, then, that I wish you to wear spectacles: — ah, hush! — you have already consented to wear then, *for my sake*. You shall accept the little toy which I now hold in my hand, and which, though admirable as an aid to vision, is really of no very immense value as a gem. You perceive that, by a trifling modification thus — or thus — it can be adapted to the eyes in the form of spectacles, or worn in the waistcoat pocket as an eyeglass. It is in the former mode, however, and habitually, that you have already consented to wear it *for my sake*."

This request — must I confess it? — confused me in no little degree. But the condition with which it was coupled rendered hesitation, of course, a matter altogether out of the question.

"It is done!" I cried, with all the enthusiasm that I could muster at the moment. "It is done — it is most cheerfully agreed. I sacrifice every feeling for your sake. To-night I wear this dear eye-glass, *as* an eye-glass, and upon my heart; but with the earliest dawn of that morning which gives me the pleasure of calling you wife, I will place it upon my — upon my nose, — and there wear it ever afterward, in the less romantic, and less fashionable, but certainly in the more serviceable, form which you desire."

Our conversation now turned upon the details of our arrangements for the morrow. Talbot, I learned from my betrothed, had just arrived in town. I was to see him at once, and procure a carriage. The *soirée* would scarcely break up before two; and by this hour the vehicle was to be at the door; when, in the confusion occasioned by the departure of the company, Madame L. could easily enter it unobserved. We were then to call at the house of a clergyman who would be in waiting; there be married, drop Talbot, and proceed on a short tour to the East; leaving the fashionable world at home to make whatever comments upon the matter it thought best.

Having planned all this, I immediately took leave, and went in search of Talbot, but, on the way, I could not refrain from stepping into a hotel, for the purpose of inspecting the miniature; and this I did by the powerful aid of the glasses. The countenance was a surpassingly beautiful one! Those large luminous eyes! — that proud Grecian nose! — those dark luxuriant curls! — "Ah!" said I, exultingly to myself, "this is indeed the speaking image of my beloved!" I turned the reverse, and discovered the words — "Eugénie

Lalande — aged twenty-seven years and seven months."

I found Talbot at home, and proceeded at once to ac-
quaint him with my good fortune. He professed excessive
astonishment, of course, but congratulated me most cor-
dially, and proffered every assistance in his power. In a
word, we carried out our arrangement to the letter; and, at
two in the morning, just ten minutes after the ceremony, I
found myself in a close carriage with Madame Lalande —
with Mrs. Simpson, I should say — and driving at a great
rate out of town, in a direction northeast by north, half-
north.

It had been determined for us by Talbot, that, as we were
to be up all night, we should make our first stop at C——,
a village about twenty miles from the city, and there get an
early breakfast and some repose, before proceeding upon
our route. At four precisely, therefore, the carraige drew up
at the door of the principal inn. I handed my adored wife
out, and ordered breakfast forthwith. In the meantime we
were shown into a small parlor, and sat down.

It was now nearly if not altogether daylight; and, as I
gazed, enraptured, at the angel by my side, the singular idea
came, all at once, into my head, that this was really the very
first moment since my acquaintance with the celebrated
loveliness of Madame Lalande, that I had enjoyed a near inspection of that loveliness by daylight at all.

"And now, *mon ami*," said she, taking my hand, and so
interrupting this train of reflection, "and now, *mon cher
ami*, since we are indissolubly one — since I have yielded to
your passionate entreaties, and performed my portion of
our agreement — I presume you have not forgotten that
you also have a little favor to bestow — a little promise
which it is your intention to keep. Ah! let me see! Let me

remember! Yes; full easily do I call to mind the precise
words of the dear promise you made to Eugénie last night.
Listen! You spoke thus: 'It is done! — it is most cheerfully
agreed! I sacrifice every feeling for your sake. To-night I
wear this dear eye-glass *as* an eye-glass, and upon my heart;
but with the earliest dawn of that morning which gives me
the privilege of calling you wife, I will place it upon my —
upon my nose, — and there wear it ever afterward, in
the less romantic, and less fashionable, but certainly in the
more serviceable, form which you desire.' These were the
exact words, my beloved husband, were they not?"

"They were," I said; "you have an excellent memory; and
assuredly, my beautiful Eugénie, there is no disposition on
my part to evade the performance of the trivial promise
they imply. See! Behold! They are becoming — rather —
are they not?" And here, having arranged the glasses in the
ordinary form of spectacles, I applied them gingerly in their
proper position; while Madame Simpson, adjusting her
cap, and folding her arms, sat bolt upright in her chair, in a
somewhat stiff and prim, and indeed, in a somewhat undig-
nified position.

"Goodness gracious me!" I exclaimed, almost at the very
instant that the rim of the spectacles had settled upon my
nose — "*My!* goodness gracious me! — why what *can* be
the matter with these glasses?" and taking them quickly off,
I wiped them carefully with a silk handkerchief and adjusted them again.

But if, in the first instance, there had occurred something
which occasioned me surprise, in the second, this surprise
became elevated into astonishment; and this astonishment
was profound — was extreme — indeed I may say it was
horrific. What, in the name of every thing hideous, did

this mean? Could I believe my eyes? — *could* I? — that was the question. Was that — was that — was that *rouge*? And were those — and were those — were those *wrinkles*, upon the visage of Eugénie Lalande? And oh! Jupiter, and every one of the gods and goddesses, little and big! — what — what — what — *what* had become of her teeth? I dashed the spectacles violently to the ground, and, leaping to my feet, stood erect in the middle of the floor, confronting Mrs. Simpson, with my arms set a-kimbo, and grinning and foaming, but, at the same time, utterly speechless with terror and with rage.

Now I have already said that Madame Eugénie Lalande — that is to say, Simpson — spoke the English language but very little better than she wrote it; and for this reason she very properly never attempted to speak it upon ordinary occasions. But rage will carry a lady to any extreme; and in the present case it carried Mrs. Simpson to the very extraordinary extreme of attempting to hold a conversation in a tongue that she did not altogether understand.

"Vell, Monsieur," said she, after surveying me, in great apparent astonishment, for some moments — "Vell, Monsieur! — and vat den? — vat de matter now? Is it de dance of de Saint Vitusse dat you ave? If not like me, vat for vy buy de pig in de poke?"

"You wretch!" said I, catching my breath — "you — you — you villainous old hag!"

"Ag? — ole? — me not so *ver* ole, after all! me not one single day more dan de eighty-doo."

"Eighty-two!" I ejaculated, staggering to the wall — "eighty-two hundred thousand baboons! The miniature said twenty-seven years and seven months!"

"To be sure! — dat is so! — ver true! but den de portraite

has been take for dese fifty-five year. Ven I go marry my segonde usbande, Monsieur Lalande, at dat time I had de portraite take for my daughter by my first usbande, Monsieur Moissart!"

"Moissart!" said I.

"Yes, Moissart," said she, mimicking my pronunciation, which, to speak the truth, was none of the best; "and vat den? Vat *you* know about de Moissart?"

"Nothing, you old fright! — I know nothing about him at all; only I had an ancestor of that name, once upon a time."

"Dat name! and vat you ave for say to dat name? 'Tis ver *goot* name; and so is Voissart — dat is ver goot name too. My daughter, Mademoiselle Moissart, she marry von Monsieur Voissart; and de name is both *ver* respectaable name."

"Moissart?" I exclaimed, "and Voissart! why what is it you mean?"

"Vat I mean? — I mean Moissart and Voissart; and for de matter of dat, I mean Croissart and Froissart, too, if I only tink proper to mean it. My daughter's daughter, Mademoiselle Voissart, she marry von Monsieur Croissart, and den agin, my daughter's grande daughter, Mademoiselle Croissart, she marry von Monsieur Froissart; and I suppose you say dat *dat* is not von *ver* respectaable name."

"Froissart!" said I, beginning to faint, "why surely you don't say Moissart, and Voissart, and Croissart, and Froissart?"

"Yes," she replied, leaning fully back in her chair, and stretching out her lower limbs at great length; "yes, Moissart, and Voissart, and Croissart, and Froissart. But Monsieur Froissart, he vas von *ver* big vat you call fool — he vas von ver great big donce like yourself — for he lef *la belle France* for come to dis stupide Amérique — and ven he get here he vent and ave von *ver* stupide, von *ver*, *ver* stupide sonn, so I hear, dough I not yet av de plaisir to meet vid him — neither me nor my companion, de Madame Stephanie Lalande. He is name de Napoleon Bonaparte Froissart, and I suppose you say dat *dat*, too, is not von *ver* respectaable name."

Either the length or the nature of this speech, had the effect of working up Mrs. Simpson into a very extraordinary passion indeed: and as she made an end of it, with great labor, she jumped up from her chair like somebody bewitched, dropping upon the floor an entire universe of bustle as she jumped. Once upon her feet, she gnashed her gums, brandished her arms, rolled up her sleeves, shook her fist in my face, and concluded the performance by tearing the cap from her head, and with it an immense wig of the most valuable and beautiful black hair, the whole of which she dashed upon the ground with a yell, and there trampled and danced a fandango upon it, in an absolute ecstasy and agony of rage.

Meantime I sank aghast into the chair which she had vacated. "Moissart and Voissart!" I repeated, thoughtfully, as she cut one of her pigeon-wings, and Croissart and Froissart!" as she completed another — "Moissart and Voissart and Croissart and Napoleon Bonaparte Froissart" — why, you ineffable old serpent, that's *me* — that's *me* — d'ye hear? — that's *me*" — here I screamed at the top of my voice — "that's *me-e-e!* I am Napoleon Bonaparte Froissart! and if I haven't married my great, great, grandmother, I wish I may be everlastingly confounded!"

Madame Eugénie Lalande, *quasi* Simpson — formerly Moissart — was, in sober fact, my great, great grandmother. In her youth she had been beautiful, and even at eighty-two, retained the majestic height, the sculptural contour of head, the fine eyes and the Grecian nose of her girlhood. By the aid of these, of pearl-powder, of rouge, of false hair, false teeth, and false *tournure*, as well as of the most skilful modistes of Paris, she contrived to hold a respectable footing among the beauties *un peu passées* of the French metropolis. In this respect, indeed, she might have been regarded as little less than the equal of the celebrated Ninon de L'Enclos.

She was immensely wealthy, and being left, for the second time, a widow without children, she bethought herself of my existence in America, and for the purpose of making me her heir, paid a visit to the United States, in company with a distant and exceedingly lovely relative of her second husband's — a Madame Stephanie Lalande.

At the opera, my great, great grandmother's attention was arrested by my notice; and, upon surveying me through her eye-glass, she was struck with a certain family resemblance to herself. Thus interested, and knowing that the heir she sought was actually in the city, she made inquiries of her party respecting me. The gentleman who attended her knew my person, and told her who I was. The information thus obtained induced her to renew her scrutiny; and this scrutiny it was which so emboldened me that I behaved in the absurd manner already detailed. She returned my bow, however, under the impression that, by some odd accident, I had discovered her identity. When, deceived by my weakness of vision, and the arts of the toilet, in respect to the age and charms of the strange lady, I demanded so enthusiastically of Talbot who she was, he concluded that I meant the younger beauty, as a matter of course, and so informed me, with perfect truth, that she was "the celebrated widow, Madame Lalande."

In the street, next morning, my great, great grandmother encountered Talbot, an old Parisian acquaintance; and the conversation, very naturally, turned upon myself. My deficiencies of vision were then explained; for these were notorious, although I was entirely ignorant of their notoriety; and my good old relative discovered, much to her chagrin that she had been deceived in supposing me aware of her identity, and that I had been merely making a fool of myself in making open love, in a theatre, to an old woman unknown. By way of punishing me for this imprudence, she concocted with Talbot a plot. He purposely kept out of my way to avoid giving me the introduction. My street inquiries about "the lovely widow, Madame Lalande," were supposed to refer to the younger lady, of course; and thus the conversation with the three gentlemen whom I encountered shortly after leaving Talbot's hotel will be easily explained, as also their allusion to Ninon de L'Enclos. I had no opportunity of seeing Madame Lalande closely during daylight, and, at her musical *soirée*, my silly weakness in refusing the aid of glasses effectually prevented me from making a discovery of her age. When "Madame Lalande" was called upon to sing, the younger lady was intended; and it was she who arose to obey the call; my great, great grandmother, to further the deception, arising at the same moment and accompanying her to the piano in the main drawing-room. Had I decided upon escorting her thither, it had been her design to suggest the propriety of my remaining where I was; but my own prudential views rendered this unnecessary. The songs which I so much admired, and which so confirmed my impression of the youth of my mistress, were executed by Madame Stephanie Lalande. The eye-glass was presented by way of adding a reproof to the hoax — a sting to the epigram of the deception. Its presentation afforded an opportunity for the lecture upon affectation with which I was so especially edified. It is almost superfluous to add that the glasses of the instrument, as worn by the old lady, had been exchanged by her for a pair better adapted to my years. They suited me, in fact to a T.

The clergyman, who merely pretended to tie the fatal knot, was a boon companion of Talbot's, and no priest. He was an excellent "whip," however; and having doffed his cassock to put on a great-coat, he drove the hack which conveyed the "happy couple" out of town. Talbot took a seat at his side. The two scoundrels were thus "in at the death," and through a half-open window of the back parlor of the inn, amused themselves in grinning at the *dénouement* of the drama. I believe I shall be forced to call them both out.

Nevertheless, I am *not* the husband of my great, great grandmother; and this is a reflection which affords me infinite relief; — but I *am* the husband of Madame Lalande — of Madame Stephanie Lalande — with whom my good old relative, besides making me her sole heir when she dies — if she ever does — has been at the trouble of concocting me a match. In conclusion: I am done forever with *billets doux,* and am never to be met with SPECTACLES.

THE OBLONG BOX

Some years ago, I engaged passage from Charleston, S.C., to the city of New York, in the fine packet-ship "Independence," Captain Hardy. We were to sail on the fifteenth of the month (June), weather permitting; and, on the fourteenth, I went on board to arrange some matters in my state-room.

I found that we were to have a great many passengers, including a more than usual number of ladies. On the list were several of my acquaintances; and among other names, I was rejoiced to see that of Mr. Cornelius Wyatt, a young artist, for whom I entertained feelings of warm friendship. He had been with me a fellow-student at C—— University, where we were very much together. He had the ordinary temperament of genius, and was a compound of misanthropy, sensibility, and enthusiasm. To these qualities he united the warmest and truest heart which ever beat in a human bosom.

I observed that his name was carded upon *three* state-rooms: and, upon again referring to the list of passengers, I found that he had engaged passage for himself, wife, and two sisters — his own. The state-rooms were sufficiently roomy, and each had two berths, one above the other. These berths, to be sure, were so exceedingly narrow as to be in-

sufficient for more than one person; still, I could not comprehend why there were *three* state-rooms for these four
persons. I was, just at that epoch, in one of those moody
frames of mind which make a man abnormally inquisitive
about trifles: and I confess, with shame, that I busied myself in a variety of ill-bred and preposterous conjectures
about this matter of the supernumerary state-room. It was
no business of mine, to be sure; but with none the less per-
tinacity did I occupy myself in attempts to resolve the
enigma. At last I reached a conclusion which wrought in me
great wonder why I had not arrived at it before. "It is a servant, of course," I said; "What a fool I am, not sooner to
have thought of so obvious a solution!" And then I again repaired to the list — but here I saw distinctly that *no* servant
was to come with the party: although, in fact, it had been
the original design to bring one — for the words "and servant" had been first written and then overscored. "Oh, extra baggage, to be sure," I now said to myself — "something
he wishes not to be put in the hold — something to be kept
under his own eye — ah, I have it — a painting or so —
and this is what he has been bargaining about with Nicolino, the Italian Jew." This idea satisfied me, and I dismissed
my curiosity for the nonce.

Wyatt's two sisters I knew very well, and most amiable
and clever girls they were. His wife he had newly married,
and I had never yet seen her. He had often talked about her
in my presence, however, and in his usual style of enthusiasm. He described her as of surpassing beauty, wit, and ac-
complishment. I was, therefore, quite anxious to make her
acquaintance.

On the day in which I visited the ship (the fourteenth),
Wyatt and party were also to visit it — so the captain in-

formed me, — and I waited on board an hour longer than
I had designed, in hope of being presented to the bride; but
then an apology came. "Mrs. W. was a little indisposed, and
would decline coming on board until to-morrow, at the
hour of sailing."

The morrow having arrived, I was going from my hotel
to the wharf, when Captain Hardy met me and said that,
"owing to circumstances" (a stupid but convenient phrase),
"he rather thought the 'Independence' would not sail for a
day or two, and that when all was ready, he would send up
and let me know." This I thought strange, for there was a
stiff southerly breeze; but as "the circumstances" were not
forthcoming, although I pumped for them with much per-
severance, I had nothing to do but to return home and di-
gest my impatience at leisure.

I did not receive the expected message from the captain
for nearly a week. It came at length, however, and I immediately went on board. The ship was crowded with passengers, and every thing was in the bustle attendant upon
making sail. Wyatt's party arrived in about ten minutes after myself. There were the two sisters, the bride, and the
artist — the latter in one of his customary fits of moody
misanthropy. I was too well used to these, however, to pay
them any special attention. He did not even introduce me
to his wife; — this courtesy devolving, per force, upon his
sister Marian — a very sweet and intelligent girl, who, in a
few hurried words, made us acquainted.

Mrs. Wyatt had been closely veiled; and when she raised
her veil, in acknowledging my bow, I confess that I was very
profoundly astonished. I should have been much more so,
however, had not long experience advised me not to trust,
with too implicit a reliance, the enthusiastic descriptions of

my friend, the artist, when indulging in comments upon the loveliness of woman. When beauty was the theme, I well knew with what facility he soared into the regions of the purely ideal.

The truth is, I could not help regarding Mrs. Wyatt as a decidedly plain-looking woman. If not positively ugly, she was not, I think, very far from it. She was dressed, however, in exquisite taste — and then I had no doubt that she had captivated my friend's heart by the more enduring graces of the intellect and soul. She said very few words, and passed at once into her state-room with Mr. W.

My old inquisitiveness now returned. There was *no* servant — *that* was a settled point. I looked, therefore, for the extra baggage. After some delay, a cart arrived at the wharf, with an oblong pine box, which was every thing that seemed to be expected. Immediately upon its arrival we made sail, and in a short time were safely over the bar and standing out to sea.

The box in question was, as I say, oblong. It was about six feet in length by two and a half in breadth; — I observed it attentively, and like to be precise. Now this shape was *peculiar*; and no sooner had I seen it, than I took credit to myself for the accuracy of my guessing. I had reached the conclusion, it will be remembered, that the extra baggage of my friend, the artist, would prove to be pictures, or at least a picture; for I knew he had been for several weeks in conference with Nicolino: — and now here was a box, which, from its shape, *could* possibly contain nothing in the world but a copy of Leonardo's "Last Supper"; and a copy of this very "Last Supper", done by Rubini the younger, at Florence, I had known, for some time, to be in the possession of Nicolino. This point, therefore, I considered as sufficiently settled. I chuckled excessively when I thought of my acumen. It was the first time I had ever known Wyatt to keep from me any of his artistical secrets; but here he evidently intended to steal a march upon me, and smuggle a fine picture to New York, under my very nose; expecting me to know nothing of the matter. I resolved to quiz him *well*, now and hereafter.

One thing, however, annoyed me not a little. The box did *not* go into the extra state-room. It was deposited in Wyatt's own; and there, too, it remained, occupying very nearly the whole of the floor — no doubt to the exceeding discomfort of the artist and his wife; — this the more especially as the tar or paint with which it was lettered in sprawling capitals, emitted a strong, disagreeable, and, to *my* fancy, a peculiarly disgusting odor. On the lid were painted the words — *"Mrs. Adelaide Curtis, Albany, New York. Charge of Cornelius Wyatt, Esq. This side up. To be handled with care."*

Now, I was aware that Mrs. Adelaide Curtis, of Albany, was the artist's wife's mother; — but then I looked upon the whole address as a mystification, intended especially for myself. I made up my mind, of course, that the box and contents would never get farther north than the studio of my misanthropic friend, in Chambers Street, New York.

For the first three or four days we had fine weather, although the wind was dead ahead; having chopped round to the northward, immediately upon our losing sight of the coast. The passengers were, consequently, in high spirits and disposed to be social. I *must* except, however, Wyatt and his sisters, who behaved stiffly, and, I could not help thinking, uncourteously to the rest of the party. *Wyatt's* conduct I did not so much regard. He was gloomy, even be-

yond his usual habit — in fact he was *morose* — but in him
I was prepared for eccentricity. For the sisters, however, I
could make no excuse. They secluded themselves in their
state-rooms during the greater part of the passage, and absolutely refused, although I repeatedly urged them, to hold
communication with any person on board.

Mrs. Wyatt herself was far more agreeable. That is to say,
she was *chatty*; and to be chatty is no slight recommenda-
tion at sea. She became *excessively* intimate with most of the
ladies; and, to my profound astonishment, evinced no
equivocal disposition to coquet with the men. She amused
us all very much. I say *"amused"* — and scarcely know how
to explain myself. The truth is, I soon found that Mrs. W.
was far oftener laughed *at* than *with*. The gentlemen said
little about her; but the ladies, in a little while, pronounced
her "a good-hearted thing, rather indifferent-looking, totally uneducated, and decidedly vulgar." The great wonder
was, how Wyatt had been entrapped into such a match.
Wealth was the general solution — but this I knew to be no
solution at all; for Wyatt had told me that she neither
brought him a dollar nor had any expectations from any
source whatever. "He had married," he said, "for love, and
for love only; and his bride was far more than worthy of his
love." When I thought of these expressions, on the part of
my friend, I confess that I felt indescribably puzzled. Could
it be possible that he was taking leave of his senses? What
else could I think? *He*, so refined, so intellectual, so fastidious, with so exquisite a perception of the faulty, and so keen
an appreciation of the beautiful! To be sure, the lady seemed
especially fond of *him* — particularly so in his absence —
when she made herself ridiculous by frequent quotations of
what had been said by her "beloved husband, Mr. Wyatt."

The word "husband" seemed forever — to use one of her own delicate expressions — forever "on the tip of her tongue." In the meantime, it was observed by all on board, that he avoided *her* in the most pointed manner, and, for the most part, shut himself up alone in his state-room, where, in fact, he might have been said to live altogether, leaving his wife at full liberty to amuse herself as she thought best, in the public society of the main cabin.

My conclusion, from what I saw and heard, was, that the artist, by some unaccountable freak of fate, or perhaps in some fit of enthusiastic and fanciful passion, had been in-duced to unite himself with a person altogether beneath him, and that the natural result, entire and speedy disgust had ensued. I pitied him from the bottom of my heart — but could not, for that reason, quite forgive his incommu-nicativeness in the matter of the "Last Supper." For this I resolved to have my revenge.

One day he came upon deck, and, taking his arm as had been my wont, I sauntered with him backward and for-ward. His gloom, however (which I considered quite natu-ral under the circumstances), seemed entirely unabated. He said little, and that moodily, and with evident effort. I ven-tured a jest or two, and he made a sickening attempt at a smile. Poor fellow! — as I thought of *his wife*, I wondered that he could have heart to put on even the semblance of mirth. At last I ventured a home thrust. I determined to commence a series of covert insinuations, or innuendoes, about the oblong box — just to let him perceive, gradually, that I was *not* altogether the butt, or victim, of his little bit of pleasant mystification. My first observation was by way of opening a masked battery. I said something about the "peculiar shape of *that* box"; and, as I spoke the words, I

smiled knowingly, winked, and touched him gently with
my forefinger in the ribs.

The manner in which Wyatt received this harmless pleas-
antry convinced me, at once, that he was mad. At first he
stared at me as if he found it impossible to comprehend
the witticism of my remark; but as its point seemed slowly
to make its way into his brain, his eyes, in the same proportion, seemed protruding from their sockets. Then he
grew very red — then hideously pale — then, as if highly
amused with what I had insinuated, he began a loud and
boisterous laugh, which, to my astonishment, he kept up,
with gradually increasing vigor, for ten minutes or more. In
conclusion, he fell flat and heavily upon the deck. When I
ran to uplift him, to all appearance he was *dead*.

I called assistance, and, with much difficulty, we brought
him to himself. Upon reviving he spoke incoherently for
some time. At length we bled him and put him to bed. The
next morning he was quite recovered, so far as regarded his
mere bodily health. Of his mind I say nothing, of course. I
avoided him during the rest of the passage, by advice of the
captain, who seemed to coincide with me altogether in my
views of his insanity, but cautioned me to say nothing on
this head to any person on board.

Several circumstances occurred immediately after this fit
of Wyatt's, which contributed to heighten the curiosity
with which I was already possessed. Among other things,
this: I had been nervous — drank too much strong green
tea, and slept ill at night — in fact, for two nights I could
not be properly said to sleep at all. Now, my state-room
opened into the main cabin, or dining-room, as did those
of all the single men on board. Wyatt's three rooms were in
the after-cabin, which was separated from the main one by

a slight sliding door, never locked even at night. As we were almost constantly on a wind, and the breeze was not a little stiff, the ship heeled to leeward very considerably; and whenever her starboard side was to leeward, the sliding door between the cabins slid open, and so remained, nobody taking the trouble to get up and shut it. But my berth was in such a position, that when my own state-room door was open, as well as the sliding door in question (and my own door was *always* open on account of the heat) I could see into the after-cabin quite distinctly, and just at that portion of it, too, where were situated the state-rooms of Mr. Wyatt. Well, during two nights (*not* consecutive) while I lay awake, I clearly saw Mrs. W., about eleven o'clock upon each night, steal cautiously from the state-room of Mr. W., and enter the extra room, where she remained until daybreak, when she was called by her husband and went back. That they were virtually separated was clear. They had separate apartments — no doubt in contemplation of a more permanent divorce; and here, after all, I thought was the mystery of the extra state-room.

There was another circumstance, too, which interested me much. During the two wakeful nights in question, and immediately after the disappearance of Mrs. Wyatt into the extra state-room, I was attracted by certain singular, cautious, subdued noises in that of her husband. After listening to them for some time, with thoughtful attention, I at length succeeded perfectly in translating their import. They were sounds occasioned by the artist in prying open the oblong box, by means of a chisel and mallet — the latter being apparently muffled, or deadened, by some soft woollen or cotton substance in which its head was enveloped.

In this manner I fancied I could distinguish the precise

moment when he fairly disengaged the lid — also, that I could determine when he removed it altogether, and when he deposited it upon the lower berth in his room; this latter point I knew, for example, by certain slight taps which the lid made in striking against the wooden edges of the berth, as he endeavored to lay it down *very* gently — there being no room for it on the floor. After this there was a dead stillness, and I heard nothing more, upon either occasion, until nearly daybreak; unless, perhaps, I may mention a low sobbing, or murmuring sound, so very much suppressed as to be nearly inaudible — if, indeed, the whole of this latter noise were not rather produced by my own imagination. I say it seemed to *resemble* sobbing or sighing — but, of course, it could not have been either. I rather think it was a ringing in my own ears. Mr. Wyatt, no doubt, according to custom, was merely giving the rein to one of his hobbies — indulging in one of his fits of artistic enthusiasm. He had opened his oblong box, in order to feast his eyes on the pictorial treasure within. There was nothing in this, however, to make him *sob*. I repeat, therefore, that it must have been simply a freak of my own fancy, distempered by good Captain Hardy's green tea. Just before dawn, on each of the two nights of which I speak, I distinctly heard Mr. Wyatt replace the lid upon the oblong box, and force the nails into their old places by means of the muffled mallet. Having done this, he issued from his state-room, fully dressed, and proceeded to call Mrs. W. from hers.

We had been at sea seven days, and were now off Cape Hatteras, when there came a tremendously heavy blow from the southwest. We were, in a measure, prepared for it, however, as the weather had been holding out threats for some time. Every thing was made snug, alow and aloft; and as the wind steadily freshened, we lay to, at length, under spanker and foretopsail, both double-reefed.

In this trim we rode safely enough for forty-eight hours — the ship proving herself an excellent sea-boat in many respects, and shipping no water of any consequence. At the end of this period, however, the gale had freshened into a hurricane, and our after-sail split into ribbons, bringing us so much in the trough of the water that we shipped several prodigious seas, one immediately after the other. By this accident we lost three men overboard with the caboose, and nearly the whole of the larboard bulwarks. Scarcely had we recovered our senses, before the foretopsail went into shreds, when we got up a storm stay-sail, and with this did pretty well for some hours, the ship heading the sea much more steadily than before.

The gale still held on, however, and we saw no signs of its abating. The rigging was found to be ill-fitted, and greatly strained; and on the third day of the blow, about five in the afternoon, our mizzen-mast, in a heavy lurch to windward, went by the board. For an hour or more, we tried in vain to get rid of it, on account of the prodigious rolling of the ship; and, before we had succeeded, the carpenter came aft and announced four feet water in the hold. To add to our dilemma, we found the pumps choked and nearly useless.

All was now confusion and despair — but an effort was made to lighten the ship by throwing overboard as much of her cargo as could be reached, and by cutting away the two masts that remained. This we at last accomplished — but we were still unable to do any thing at the pumps: and, in the meantime, the leak gained on us very fast.

At sundown, the gale had sensibly diminished in vio-

lence, and, as the sea went down with it, we still entertained
faint hopes of saving ourselves in the boats. At eight P.M.,
the clouds broke away to windward, and we had the ad-
vantage of a full moon — a piece of good fortune which
served wonderfully to cheer our drooping spirits.

After incredible labor we succeeded, at length, in getting
the long-boat over the side without material accident, and
into this we crowded the whole of the crew and most of the
passengers. This party made off immediately, and, after un-
dergoing much suffering, finally arrived, in safety, at Ocra-
coke Inlet, on the third day after the wreck.

Fourteen passengers, with the captain, remained on
board, resolving to trust their fortunes to the jolly-boat at
the stern. We lowered it without difficulty, although it was
only by a miracle that we prevented it from swamping as it
touched the water. It contained, when afloat, the captain
and his wife, Mr. Wyatt and party, a Mexican officer, wife,
four children, and myself, with a negro valet.

We had no room, of course, for any thing except a few
positively necessary instruments, some provisions, and the
clothes upon our backs. No one had thought of even attempting to save any thing more. What must have been the
astonishment of all, then, when, having proceeded a few
fathoms from the ship, Mr. Wyatt stood up in the stern-
sheets, and coolly demanded of Captain Hardy that the
boat should be put back for the purpose of taking in his oblong box!

"Sit down, Mr. Wyatt," replied the captain, somewhat
sternly, "you will capsize us if you do not sit quite still. Our
gunwale is almost in the water now."

"The box!" vociferated Mr. Wyatt, still standing — "the
box, I say! Captain Hardy, you cannot, you *will* not refuse

me. Its weight will be but a trifle — it is nothing — mere nothing. By the mother who bore you — for the love of Heaven — by your hope of salvation, I *implore* you to put back for the box!"

The captain, for a moment, seemed touched by the earnest appeal of the artist, but he regained his stern composure, and merely said:

"Mr. Wyatt, you are *mad*. I cannot listen to you. Sit down, I say, or you will swamp the boat. Stay — hold him — seize him! — he is about to spring overboard! There — I knew it — he is over!"

As the captain said this, Mr. Wyatt, in fact, sprang from the boat, and, as we were yet in the lee of the wreck, succeeded, by almost superhuman exertion, in getting hold of a rope which hung from the fore-chains. In another moment he was on board, and rushing frantically down into the cabin.

In the meantime, we had been swept astern of the ship, and being quite out of her lee, were at the mercy of the tremendous sea which was still running. We made a determined effort to put back, but our little boat was like a feather in the breath of the tempest. We saw at a glance that the doom of the unfortunate artist was sealed.

As our distance from the wreck rapidly increased, the madman (for as such only could we regard him) was seen to emerge from the companionway, up which by dint of strength that appeared gigantic, he dragged, bodily, the oblong box. While we gazed in the extremity of astonishment, he passed, rapidly, several turns of a three-inch rope, first around the box and then around his body. In another instant both body and box were in the sea — disappearing suddenly, at once and forever.

We lingered awhile sadly upon our oars, with our eyes riveted upon the spot. At length we pulled away. The silence remained unbroken for an hour. Finally, I hazarded a remark.

"Did you observe, Captain, how suddenly they sank? Was not that an exceedingly singular thing? I confess that I entertained some feeble hope of his final deliverance, when I saw him lash himself to the box, and commit himself to the sea."

"They sank as a matter of course," replied the captain, "and that like a shot. They will soon rise again, however — *but not till the salt melts.*"

"The salt!" I ejaculated.

"Hush!" said the captain, pointing to the wife and sisters of the deceased. "We must talk of these things at some more appropriate time."

We suffered much, and made a narrow escape; but fortune befriended *us*, as well as our mates in the long-boat. We landed, in fine, more dead than alive, after four days of intense distress, upon the beach opposite Roanoke Island. We remained here a week, were not ill-treated by the wreckers, and at length obtained a passage to New York.

About a month after the loss of the "Independence," I happened to meet Captain Hardy in Broadway. Our conversation turned, naturally, upon the disaster, and especially upon the sad fate of poor Wyatt. I thus learned the following particulars.

The artist had engaged passage for himself, wife, two sisters and a servant. His wife was, indeed, as she had been represented, a most lovely, and most accomplished woman. On the morning of the fourteenth of June (the day in

which I first visited the ship), the lady suddenly sickened
and died. The young husband was frantic with grief — but
circumstances imperatively forbade the deferring his voyage
to New York. It was necessary to take to her mother the
corpse of his adored wife, and, on the other hand, the uni-
versal prejudice which would prevent his doing so openly
was well known. Nine tenths of the passengers would have
abandoned the ship rather than take passage with a dead
body.

In this dilemma, Captain Hardy arranged that the
corpse, being first partially embalmed, and packed, with a
large quantity of salt, in a box of suitable dimensions,
should be conveyed on board as merchandise. Nothing was
to be said of the lady's decease; and, as it was well understood that Mr. Wyatt had engaged passage for his wife, it
became necessary that some person should personate her
during the voyage. This the deceased's lady's-maid was easily prevailed on to do. The extra state-room, originally engaged for this girl, during her mistress' life, was now merely
retained. In this state-room the pseudo-wife slept, of
course, every night. In the daytime she performed, to the
best of her ability, the part of her mistress — whose person,
it had been carefully ascertained, was unknown to any of
the passengers on board.

My own mistake arose, naturally enough, through too
careless, too inquisitive, and too impulsive a temperament.
But of late, it is a rare thing that I sleep soundly at night.
There is a countenance which haunts me, turn as I will.
There is an hysterical laugh which will forever ring within
my ears.

The Premature Burial

There are certain themes of which the interest is all-absorbing, but which are too entirely horrible for the purposes of legitimate fiction. These the mere romanticist must eschew, if he do not wish to offend, or to disgust. They are with propriety handled only when the severity and majesty of truth sanctify and sustain them. We thrill, for example, with the most intense of "pleasurable pain" over the accounts of the Passage of the Beresina, of the Earthquake at Lisbon, of the Plague at London, of the Massacre of St. Bartholomew, or of the stifling of the hundred and twenty-three prisoners in the Black Hole at Calcutta. But, in these accounts, it is the fact — it is the reality — it is the history which excites. As inventions, we should regard them with simple abhorrence.

I have mentioned some few of the more prominent and august calamities on record; but in these it is the extent, not less than the character of the calamity, which so vividly impresses the fancy. I need not remind the reader that, from the long and weird catalogue of human miseries, I might have selected many individual instances more replete with essential suffering than any of these vast generalities of disaster. The true wretchedness, indeed, — the ultimate woe, — is particular, not diffuse. That the ghastly extremes of agony are endured by man the unit, and never by man the mass — for this let us thank a merciful God!

To be buried while alive is, beyond question, the most terrific of these extremes which has ever fallen to the lot of mere mortality. That it has frequently, very frequently, so fallen will scarcely be denied by those who think. The boundaries which divide Life from Death are at best shadowy and vague. Who shall say where the one ends, and where the other begins? We know that there are diseases in which occur total cessations of all the apparent functions of vitality, and yet in which these cessations are merely suspensions, properly so called. They are only temporary pauses in the incomprehensible mechanism. A certain period elapses, and some unseen mysterious principle again sets in motion the magic pinions and the wizard wheels. The silver cord was not for ever loosed, nor the golden bowl irreparably broken. But where, meantime, was the soul?

Apart, however, from the inevitable conclusion, *a priori* that such causes must produce such effects, — that the well-known occurrence of such cases of suspended animation must naturally give rise, now and then, to premature interments, — apart from this consideration, we have the direct testimony of medical and ordinary experience to prove that a vast number of such interments have actually taken place. I might refer at once, if necessary, to a hundred well-authenticated instances. One of very remarkable character, and of which the circumstances may be fresh in the memory of some of my readers, occurred, not very long ago, in the neighboring city of Baltimore, where it occasioned a painful, intense, and widely-extended excitement. The wife of one of the most respectable citizens — a lawyer of eminence and a member of Congress — was seized with a sudden and unaccountable illness, which completely baffled the skill of her physicians. After much suffering she died, or was supposed to die. No one suspected, indeed, or had reason to suspect, that she was not actually dead. She presented all the ordinary appearances of death. The face assumed the usual pinched and sunken outline. The lips were of the usual marble pallor. The eyes were lustreless. There was no warmth. Pulsation had ceased. For three days the body was preserved unburied, during which it had acquired a stony rigidity. The funeral, in short, was hastened, on account of the rapid advance of what was supposed to be decomposition.

The lady was deposited in her family vault, which, for three subsequent years, was undisturbed. At the expiration of this term it was opened for the reception of a sarcophagus; — but, alas! how fearful a shock awaited the husband, who, personally, threw open the door! As its portals swung outwardly back, some white-apparelled object fell rattling within his arms. It was the skeleton of his wife in her yet unmoulded shroud.

A careful investigation rendered it evident that she had revived within two days after her entombment; that her struggles within the coffin had caused it to fall from a ledge, or shelf, to the floor, where it was so broken as to permit her escape. A lamp which had been accidentally left, full of oil, within the tomb, was found empty; it might have been exhausted, however, by evaporation. On the uppermost of the steps which led down into the dread chamber was a large fragment of the coffin, with which, it seemed that she had endeavored to arrest attention by striking the iron door. While thus occupied, she probably swooned, or possibly died, through sheer terror; and, in falling, her shroud became entangled in some iron-work which projected interiorly. Thus she remained, and thus she rotted, erect.

In the year 1810, a case of living inhumation happened in France, attended with circumstances which go far to warrant the assertion that truth is, indeed, stranger than fiction. The heroine of the story was a Mademoiselle Victorine Lafourcade, a young girl of illustrious family, of wealth, and of great personal beauty. Among her numerous suitors was Julien Bossuet, a poor *litterateur*, or journalist, of Paris. His talents and general amiability had recommended him to the notice of the heiress, by whom he seems to have been truly beloved; but her pride of birth decided her, finally, to reject him, and to wed a Monsieur Renelle, a banker and a diplomatist of some eminence. After marriage, however, this gentleman neglected, and, perhaps, even more positively ill-treated her. Having passed with him some wretched years, she died — at least her condition so closely resembled death as to deceive every one who saw her. She was buried — not in a vault, but in an ordinary grave in the village of her nativity. Filled with despair, and still inflamed by the memory of a profound attachment, the lover journeys from the capital to the remote province in which the village lies, with the romantic purpose of disinterring the corpse, and possessing himself of its luxuriant tresses. He reaches the grave. At midnight he unearths the coffin, opens it, and is in the act of detaching the hair, when he is arrested by the unclosing of the beloved eyes. In fact, the lady had been buried alive. Vitality had not altogether departed, and she was aroused by the caresses of her lover from the lethargy which had been mistaken for death. He bore her frantically to his lodgings in the village. He employed certain powerful restoratives suggested by no little medical learning. In fine, she revived. She recognized her preserver. She remained with him until, by slow degrees, she fully recovered her original health. Her woman's heart was not adamant, and this last lesson of love sufficed to soften it. She bestowed it upon Bossuet. She returned no more to her husband, but, concealing from him her resurrection, fled with her lover to America. Twenty years afterward, the two returned to France, in the persuasion that time had so greatly altered the lady's appearance that her friends would be unable to recognize her. They were mistaken, however; for, at the first meeting, Monsieur Renelle did actually recognize and make claim to his wife. This claim she resisted, and a judicial tribunal sustained her in her resistance, deciding that the peculiar circumstances, with the long lapse of years, had extinguished, not only equitably, but legally, the authority of the husband.

The *Chirurgical Journal* of Leipsic, a periodical of high authority and merit, which some American bookseller would do well to translate and republish, records in a late number a very distressing event of the character in question.

An officer of artillery, a man of gigantic stature and of robust health, being thrown from an unmanageable horse, received a very severe contusion upon the head, which rendered him insensible at once; the skull was slightly fractured, but no immediate danger was apprehended. Trepanning was accomplished successfully. He was bled, and many other of the ordinary means of relief were adopted. Gradually, however, he fell into a more and more hopeless state of stupor, and, finally, it was thought that he died.

The weather was warm, and he was buried with indecent haste in one of the public cemeteries. His funeral took place on Thursday. On the Sunday following, the grounds of the cemetery were, as usual, much thronged with visitors, and about noon an intense excitement was created by the declaration of a peasant that, while sitting upon the grave of the officer, he had distinctly felt a commotion of the earth, as if occasioned by some one struggling beneath. At first little attention was paid to the man's asseveration; but his evident terror, and the dogged obstinacy with which he persisted in his story, had at length their natural effect upon the crowd. Spades were hurriedly procured, and the grave, which was shamefully shallow, was in a few minutes so far thrown open that the head of its occupant appeared. He was then seemingly dead; but he sat nearly erect within his coffin, the lid of which, in his furious struggles, he had partially uplifted.

He was forthwith conveyed to the nearest hospital, and there pronounced to be still living, although in an asphytic condition. After some hours he revived, recognized individuals of his acquaintance, and, in broken sentences spoke of his agonies in the grave.

From what he related, it was clear that he must have been conscious of life for more than an hour, while inhumed, before lapsing into insensibility. The grave was carelessly and loosely filled with an exceedingly porous soil; and thus some air was necessarily admitted. He heard the footsteps of the crowd overhead, and endeavored to make himself heard in turn. It was the tumult within the grounds of the cemetery, he said, which appeared to awaken him from a deep sleep, but no sooner was he awake than he became fully aware of the awful horrors of his position.

This patient, it is recorded, was doing well, and seemed to be in a fair way of ultimate recovery, but fell a victim to the quackeries of medical experiment. The galvanic battery was applied, and he suddenly expired in one of those ecstatic paroxysms which, occasionally, it superinduces.

The mention of the galvanic battery, nevertheless, recalls to my memory a well-known and very extraordinary case in point, where its action proved the means of restoring to animation a young attorney of London, who had been interred for two days. This occurred in 1831, and created, at the time, a very profound sensation wherever it was made the subject of converse.

The patient, Mr. Edward Stapleton, had died, apparently, of typhus fever, accompanied with some anomalous symptoms which had excited the curiosity of his medical attendants. Upon his seeming decease, his friends were requested to sanction a *post-mortem* examination, but declined to permit it. As often happens, when such refusals are made, the practitioners resolved to disinter the body and dissect it at leisure, in private. Arrangements were easily effected with some of the numerous corps of body-snatchers with which London abounds; and, upon the third night after the funeral, the supposed corpse was unearthed from a grave eight feet deep, and deposited in the operating chamber of one of the private hospitals.

An incision of some extent had been actually made in the abdomen, when the fresh and undecayed appearance of the subject suggested an application of the battery. One experiment succeeded another, and the customary effects supervened, with nothing to characterize them in any respect, except, upon one or two occasions, a more than ordinary degree of life-likeness in the convulsive action.

It grew late. The day was about to dawn; and it was thought expedient, at length, to proceed at once to the dissection. A student, however, was especially desirous of testing a theory of his own, and insisted upon applying the battery to one of the pectoral muscles. A rough gash was made, and a wire hastily brought in contact; when the patient, with a hurried but quite unconvulsive movement, arose from the table, stepped into the middle of the floor, gazed about him uneasily for a few seconds, and then — spoke. What he said was unintelligible; but words were uttered; the syllabification was distinct. Having spoken, he fell heavily to the floor.

For some moments all were paralyzed with awe — but the urgency of the case soon restored them their presence of mind. It was seen that Mr. Stapleton was alive, although in a swoon. Upon exhibition of ether he revived and was rapidly restored to health, and to the society of his friends — from whom, however, all knowledge of his resuscitation was withheld, until a relapse was no longer to be apprehended. Their wonder — their rapturous astonishment — may be conceived.

The most thrilling peculiarity of this incident, nevertheless, is involved in what Mr. S. himself asserts. He declares that at no period was he altogether insensible — that, dully and confusedly, he was aware of everything which happened to him, from the moment in which he was pronounced *dead* by his physicians, to that in which he fell swooning to the floor of the hospital. "I am alive," were the uncomprehended words which, upon recognizing the locality of the dissecting-room, he had endeavored, in his extremity, to utter.

It were an easy matter to multiply such histories as these — but I forbear — for, indeed, we have no need of such to establish the fact that premature interments occur. When we reflect how very rarely, from the nature of the case, we have it in our power to detect them, we must admit that they may *frequently* occur without our cognizance. Scarcely, in truth, is a graveyard ever encroached upon, for any purpose, to any great extent, that skeletons are not found in postures which suggest the most fearful of suspicions.

Fearful indeed the suspicion — but more fearful the doom! It may be asserted, without hesitation, that *no* event is so terribly well adapted to inspire the supremeness of bodily and of mental distress, as is burial before death. The unendurable oppression of the lungs — the stifling fumes of the damp earth — the clinging to the death garments — the rigid embrace of the narrow house — the blackness of the absolute Night — the silence like a sea that overwhelms — the unseen but palpable presence of the Conqueror Worm — these things, with the thoughts of the air and grass above, with memory of dear friends who would fly to save us if but informed of our fate, and with consciousness that of this fate they can *never* be informed — that our hopeless portion is that of the really dead — these considerations, I say, carry into the heart, which still palpitates, a degree of appalling and intolerable horror from which the most daring imagination must recoil. We know of nothing so agonizing upon Earth — we can dream of nothing half so hideous in the realms of the nethermost Hell. And thus all narratives upon this topic have an interest profound; an interest, nevertheless, which, through the sacred awe of the topic itself, very properly and very peculiarly depends upon our conviction of the *truth* of the matter narrated. What I have now to tell is of my own actual knowledge — of my own positive and personal experience.

For several years I had been subject to attacks of the singular disorder which physicians have agreed to term catalepsy, in default of a more definite title. Although both the immediate and the predisposing causes, and even the actual diagnosis, of this disease are still mysterious, its obvious and apparent character is sufficiently well understood. Its variations seem to be chiefly of degree. Sometimes the patient lies, for a day only, or even for a shorter period, in a species of exaggerated lethargy. He is senseless and externally motionless; but the pulsation of the heart is still faintly perceptible; some traces of warmth remain; a slight color lingers within the centre of the cheek; and, upon application of a mirror to the lips, we can detect a torpid, unequal, and vacillating action of the lungs. Then again the duration of the trance is for weeks — even for months; while the closest scrutiny, and the most rigorous medical tests, fail to establish any material distinction between the state of the sufferer and what we conceive of absolute death. Very usually he is saved from premature interment solely by the knowledge of his friends that he has been previously subject to catalepsy, by the consequent suspicion excited, and, above all, by the non-appearance of decay. The advances of the malady are, luckily, gradual. The first manifestations, although marked, are unequivocal. The fits grow successively more and more distinctive, and endure each for a longer term than the preceding. In this lies the principal security from inhumation. The unfortunate whose *first* attack should be of the extreme character which is occasionally seen, would almost inevitably be consigned alive to the tomb.

My own case differed in no important particular from those mentioned in medical books. Sometimes, without any apparent cause, I sank, little by little, into a condition of semi-syncope, or half swoon; and, in this condition, without pain, without ability to stir, or, strictly speaking, to think, but with a dull lethargic consciousness of life and of the presence of those who surrounded my bed, I remained, until the crisis of the disease restored me, suddenly, to perfect sensation. At other times I was quickly and impetuously smitten. I grew sick, and numb, and chilly, and dizzy, and so fell prostrate at once. Then, for weeks, all was void, and black, and silent, and Nothing became the universe. Total annihilation could be no more. From these latter attacks I awoke, however, with a gradation slow in proportion to the suddenness of the seizure. Just as the day dawns to the friendless and houseless beggar who roams the streets throughout the long desolate winter night — just so tardily — just so wearily — just so cheerily came back the light of the Soul to me.

Apart from the tendency to trance, however, my general health appeared to be good; nor could I perceive that it was at all affected by the one prevalent malady — unless, indeed, an idiosyncrasy in my ordinary *sleep* may be looked upon as superinduced. Upon awaking from slumber, I could never gain, at once, thorough possession of my senses, and always remained, for many minutes, in much bewilderment and perplexity — the mental faculties in general, but the memory in especial, being in a condition of absolute abeyance.

In all that I endured there was no physical suffering, but of moral distress an infinitude. My fancy grew charnel. I talked "of worms, of tombs, and epitaphs." I was lost in reveries of death, and the idea of premature burial held continual possession of my brain. The ghastly Danger to which I was subjected haunted me day and night. In the former, the torture of meditation was excessive; in the latter, supreme. When the grim Darkness overspread the Earth, then, with every horror of thought, I shook — shook as the quivering plumes upon the hearse. When Nature could endure wakefulness no longer, it was with a struggle that I consented to sleep — for I shuddered to reflect that, upon awaking, I might find myself the tenant of a grave. And when, finally, I sank into slumber, it was only to rush at once into a world of phantasms, above which, with vast, sable, overshadowing wings, hovered, predominant, the one sepulchral Idea.

From the innumerable images of gloom which thus oppressed me in dreams, I select for record but a solitary vision. Methought I was immersed in a cataleptic trance of more than usual duration and profundity. Suddenly there came an icy hand upon my forehead, and an impatient, gibbering voice whispered the word "Arise!" within my ear.

I sat erect. The darkness was total. I could not see the figure of him who had aroused me. I could call to mind neither the period at which I had fallen into the trance, nor the locality in which I then lay. While I remained motionless, and busied in endeavors to collect my thoughts, the cold hand grasped me fiercely by the wrist, shaking it petulantly, while the gibbering voice said again:

"Arise! did I not bid thee arise?"

"And who," I demanded, "art thou?"

"I have no name in the regions which I inhabit," replied the voice, mournfully; "I was mortal, but am fiend. I was merciless, but am pitiful. Thou dost feel that I shudder. My teeth chatter as I speak, yet it is not with the chilliness of the night — of the night without end. But this hideousness is insufferable. How canst *thou* tranquilly sleep? I cannot rest for the cry of these great agonies. These sights are more than I can bear. Get thee up! Come with me into the outer Night, and let me unfold to thee the graves. Is not this a spectacle of woe? — Behold!"

I looked; and the unseen figure, which still grasped me by the wrist, had caused to be thrown open the graves of all mankind; and from each issued the faint phosphoric radiance of decay; so that I could see into the innermost recesses, and there view the shrouded bodies in their sad and solemn slumbers with the worm. But alas! the real sleepers were fewer, by many millions, than those who slumbered not at all; and there was a feeble struggling; and there was a general and sad unrest; and from out the depths of the countless pits there came a melancholy rustling from the garments of the buried. And of those who seemed tranquilly to repose, I saw that a vast number had changed, in a greater or less degree, the rigid and uneasy position in which they had originally been entombed. And the voice again said to me as I gazed:

"Is it not — oh! is it *not* a pitiful sight?" But, before I could find words to reply, the figure had ceased to grasp my wrist, the phosphoric lights expired, and the graves were closed with a sudden violence, while from out them arose a tumult of despairing cries, saying again: "Is it not — O, God! is it *not* a very pitiful sight?"

Phantasies such as these, presenting themselves at night, extended their terrific influence far into my waking hours. My nerves became thoroughly unstrung, and I fell a prey to perpetual horror. I hesitated to ride, or to walk, or to indulge in any exercise that would carry me from home. In fact, I no longer dared trust myself out of the immediate presence of those who were aware of my proneness to catalepsy, lest, falling into one of my usual fits, I should be buried before my real condition could be ascertained. I doubted the care, the fidelity of my dearest friends. I dreaded that, in some trance of more than customary duration, they might be prevailed upon to regard me as irrecoverable. I even went so far as to fear that, as I occasioned much trouble, they might be glad to consider any very protracted attack as sufficient excuse for getting rid of me altogether. It was in vain they endeavored to reassure me by the most solemn promises. I exacted the most sacred oaths, that under no circumstances they would bury me until decomposition had so materially advanced as to render further preservation impossible. And, even then, my mortal terrors would listen to no reason — would accept no consolation. I entered into a series of elaborate precautions. Among other things, I had the family vault so remodelled as to admit of being readily opened from within. The slightest pressure upon a long lever that extended far into the tomb would cause the iron portals to fly back. There were arrangements also for the free admission of air and light, and convenient receptacles for food and water, within immediate reach of the coffin intended for my reception. This coffin was warmly and softly padded, and was provided with a lid, fashioned upon the principle of the vault-door, with the addition of springs so contrived that the feeblest movement of the body would be sufficient to set it at liberty. Besides all this, there was suspended from the roof of the tomb, a large bell, the rope of which, it was designed, should extend through a hole in the coffin, and so be fastened to one of the hands of the corpse. But, alas! what avails the vigilance against the Destiny of man? Not even these well-contrived securities sufficed to save from the uttermost agonies of living inhumation, a wretch to these agonies foredoomed!

There arrived an epoch — as often before there had arrived — in which I found myself emerging from total unconsciousness into the first feeble and indefinite sense of existence. Slowly — with a tortoise gradation — approached the faint gray dawn of the psychal day. A torpid uneasiness. An apathetic endurance of dull pain. No care — no hope — no effort. Then, after a long interval, a ringing in the ears; then, after a lapse still longer, a pricking or tingling sensation in the extremities; then a seemingly eternal period of pleasurable quiescence, during which the awakening feelings are struggling into thought; then a brief re-sinking into non-entity; then a sudden recovery. At length the slight quivering of an eyelid, and immediately thereupon, an electric shock of a terror, deadly and indefinite, which sends the blood in torrents from the temples to the heart. And now the first positive effort to think. And now the first endeavor to remember. And now a partial and evanescent success. And now the memory has so far regained its dominion, that, in some measure, I am cognizant of my state. I feel that I am not awaking from ordinary sleep. I recollect that I have been subject to catalepsy. And now, at last, as if by the rush of an ocean, my shuddering spirit is overwhelmed by the one grim Danger — by the one spectral and ever-prevalent idea.

For some minutes after this fancy possessed me, I remained without motion. And why? I could not summon courage to move. I dared not make the effort which was to satisfy me of my fate — and yet there was something at my heart which whispered me *it was sure*. Despair — such as no other species of wretchedness ever calls into being — despair alone urged me, after long irresolution, to uplight the heavy lids of my eyes. I uplifted them. It was dark — all dark. I knew that the fit was over. I knew that the crisis of my disorder had long passed. I knew that I had now fully recovered the use of my visual faculties — and yet it was dark — all dark — the intense and utter raylessness of the Night that endureth for evermore.

I endeavored to shriek; and my lips and my parched tongue moved convulsively together in the attempt — but no voice issued from the cavernous lungs, which, oppressed as if by the weight of some incumbent mountain, gasped and palpitated, with the heart, at every elaborate and struggling inspiration.

The movement of the jaws, in this effort to cry aloud, showed me that they were bound up, as is usual with the dead. I felt, too, that I lay upon some hard substance; and by something similar my sides were, also, closely compressed. So far, I had not ventured to stir any of my limbs — but now I violently threw up my arms, which had been lying at length, with the wrists crossed. They struck a solid wooden substance, which extended above my person at an elevation of not more than six inches from my face. I could no longer doubt that I reposed within a coffin at last.

And now, amid all my infinite miseries, came sweetly the cherub Hope — for I thought of my precautions. I writhed, and made spasmodic exertions to force open the lid: it would not move. I felt my wrists for the bell-rope: it was not to be found. And now the Comforter fled for ever, and a still sterner Despair reigned triumphant; for I could not help perceiving the absence of the paddings which I had so carefully prepared — and then, too, there came suddenly to my nostrils the strong peculiar odor of moist earth. The conclusion was irresistible. I was *not* within the vault. I had fallen into a trance while absent from home — while among strangers — when, or how, I could not remember — and it was they who had buried me as a dog — nailed up in some common coffin — and thrust, deep, deep, and for ever, into some ordinary and nameless *grave*.

As this awful conviction forced itself, thus, into the innermost chambers of my soul, I once again struggled to cry aloud. And in this second endeavor I succeeded. A long, wild, and continuous shriek, or yell, of agony, resounded through the realms of the subterranean Night.

"Hillo! hillo, there!" said a gruff voice, in reply.

"What the devil's the matter now!" said a second.

"Get out o' that!" said a third.

"What do you mean by yowling in that ere kind of style, like a cattymount?" said a fourth; and hereupon I was seized and shaken without ceremony, for several minutes, by a junto of very rough-looking individuals. They did not arouse me from my slumber — for I was wide-awake when I screamed — but they restored me to the full possession of my memory.

This adventure occurred near Richmond, in Virginia. Accompanied by a friend, I had proceeded, upon a gunning expedition, some miles down the banks of the James River. Night approached, and we were overtaken by a storm. The cabin of a small sloop lying at anchor in the stream, and laden with garden mould, afforded us the only available shelter. We made the best of it, and passed the night on board. I slept in one of the only two berths in the vessel — and the berths of a sloop of sixty or seventy tons need scarcely be described. That which I occupied had no bedding of any kind. Its extreme width was eighteen inches.

The distance of its bottom from the deck overhead was precisely the same. I found it a matter of exceeding difficulty to squeeze myself in. Nevertheless, I slept soundly; and the whole of my vision — for it was no dream, and no nightmare — arose naturally from the circumstances of my position — from my ordinary bias of thought — and from the difficulty, to which I have alluded, of collecting my senses, and especially of regaining my memory, for a long time after awaking from slumber. The men who shook me were the crew of the sloop, and some laborers engaged to unload it. From the load itself came the earthy smell. The bandage about the jaws was a silk handkerchief in which I had bound up my head, in default of my customary nightcap.

The tortures endured, however, were indubitably quite equal, for the time, to those of actual sepulture. They were fearfully — they were inconceivably hideous; but out of Evil proceeded Good; for their very excess wrought in my spirit an inevitable revulsion. My soul acquired tone — acquired temper. I went abroad. I took vigorous exercise. I breathed the free air of Heaven. I thought upon other subjects than Death. I discarded my medical books. "Buchan" I burned. I read no "Night Thoughts" — no fustian about church-yards — no bugaboo tales — *such as this.* In short I became a new man, and lived a man's life. From that memorable night, I dismissed forever my charnel apprehensions, and with them vanished the cataleptic disorder, of which, perhaps, they had been less the consequence than the cause.

There are moments when, even to the sober eye of Reason, the world of our sad Humanity may assume the semblance of a Hell — but the imagination of man is no Carathis, to explore with impunity its every cavern. Alas!

THE OVAL PORTRAIT

The château into which my valet had ventured to make forcible entrance, rather than permit me, in my desperately wounded condition, to pass a night in the open air, was one of those piles of commingled gloom and grandeur which have so long frowned among the Apennines, not less in fact than in the fancy of Mrs. Radcliffe. To all appearance it had been temporarily and very lately abandoned. We established ourselves in one of the smallest and least sumptuously furnished apartments. It lay in a remote turret of the building. Its decorations were rich, yet tattered and antique. Its walls were hung with tapestry and bedecked with manifold and multiform armorial trophies, together with an unusually great number of very spirited modern paintings in frames of rich golden arabesque. In these paintings, which depended from the walls not only in their main surfaces, but in very many nooks which the bizarre architecture of the château rendered necessary — in these paintings my incipient delirium, perhaps, had caused me to take deep interest; so that I bade Pedro to close the heavy shutters of the room — since it was already night, — to light the tongues of a tall candelabrum which stood by the head of my bed, and to throw open far and wide the fringed curtains of black velvet which enveloped the bed itself. I wished all this done that I might resign myself, if not to sleep, at least alternately to the contemplation of these pictures, and the perusal of a small volume which had been found upon the pillow, and which purported to criticise and describe them.

Long, long I read — and devoutly, devoutly I gazed. Rapidly and gloriously the hours flew by and the deep midnight came. The position of the candelabrum displeased me, and outreaching my hand with difficulty, rather than disturb my slumbering valet, I placed it so as to throw its rays more fully upon the book.

But the action produced an effect altogether unanticipated. The rays of the numerous candles (for there were many) now fell within a niche of the room which had hitherto been thrown into deep shade by one of the bedposts. I thus saw in vivid light a picture all unnoticed before. It was the portrait of a young girl just ripening into womanhood. I glanced at the painting hurriedly, and then closed my eyes. Why I did this was not at first apparent even to my own perception. But while my lids remained thus shut, I ran over in mind my reason for so shutting them. It was an impulsive movement to gain time for thought — to make sure that my vision had not deceived me — to calm and subdue my fancy for a more sober and more certain gaze. In a very few moments I again looked fixedly at the painting.

That I now saw aright I could not and would not doubt; for the first flashing of the candles upon that canvas had seemed to dissipate the dreamy stupor which was stealing over my senses, and to startle me at once into waking life.

The portrait, I have already said, was that of a young girl. It was a mere head and shoulders, done in what is technically termed a *vignette* manner; much in the style of the favorite heads of Sully. The arms, the bosom, and even the ends of the radiant hair melted imperceptibly into the vague yet deep shadow which formed the background of the whole. The frame was oval, richly gilded and filigreed in *Moresque*. As a thing of art nothing could be more admirable than the painting itself. But it could have been neither the execution of the work, nor the immortal beauty of the countenance, which had so suddenly and so vehemently moved me. Least of all, could it have been that my fancy, shaken from its half slumber, had mistaken the head for that of a living person. I saw at once that the peculiarities of the design, of the *vignetting*, and of the frame, must have instantly dispelled such idea — must have prevented even its momentary entertainment. Thinking earnestly upon these points, I remained, for an hour perhaps, half sitting, half reclining, with my vision riveted upon the portrait. At length, satisfied with the true secret of its effect, I fell back within the bed. I had found the spell of the picture in an absolute *life-likeliness* of expression, which, at first startling, finally confounded, subdued, and appalled me. With deep and reverent awe I replaced the candelabrum in its former position. The cause of my deep agitation being thus shut from view, I sought eagerly the volume which discussed the paintings and their histories. Turning to the number which designated the oval portrait, I there read the vague and quaint words which follow:

"She was a maiden of rarest beauty, and not more lovely than full of glee. And evil was the hour when she saw, and loved, and wedded the painter. He, passionate, studious, austere, and having already a bride in his Art: she a maiden of rarest beauty, and not more lovely than full of glee; all light and smiles, and frolicsome as the young fawn; loving and cherishing all things; hating only the Art which was her

rival; dreading only the pallet and brushes and other unto-
ward instruments which deprived her of the countenance of
her lover. It was thus a terrible thing for this lady to hear the
painter speak of his desire to portray even his young bride.
But she was humble and obedient, and sat meekly for many
weeks in the dark high turret-chamber where the light
dripped upon the pale canvas only from overhead. But he,
the painter, took glory in his work, which went on from
hour to hour, and from day to day. And he was a passionate, and wild, and moody man, who became lost in reveries; so that he *would* not see that the light which fell so
ghastly in that lone turret withered the health and the spirits of his bride, who pined visibly to all but him. Yet she
smiled on and still on, uncomplainingly, because she saw
that the painter (who had high renown) took a fervid and
burning pleasure in his task, and wrought day and night to
depict her who so loved him, yet who grew daily more
dispirited and weak. And in sooth some who beheld the
portrait spoke of its resemblance in low words, as of a
mighty marvel, and a proof not less of the power of the
painter than of his deep love for her whom he depicted so
surpassingly well. But at length, as the labor drew nearer to
its conclusion, there were admitted none into the turret; for
the painter had grown wild with the ardor of his work, and
turned his eyes from the canvas rarely, even to regard the
countenance of his wife. And he *would* not see that the tints
which he spread upon the canvas were drawn from the
cheeks of her who sat beside him. And when many weeks
had passed, and but little remained to do, save one brush
upon the mouth and one tint upon the eye, the spirit of the
lady again flickered up as the flame within the socket of the
lamp. And then the brush was given, and then the tint was

placed; and, for one moment, the painter stood entranced before the work which he had wrought; but in the next, while he yet gazed, he grew tremulous and very pallid, and aghast, and crying with a loud voice, 'This is indeed *Life* itself!' turned suddenly to regard his beloved: — *She was dead!*"

MORELLA

Αυτο χαϑ' αυτο μεϑ' αυτου, μουο ειδες αιει ου.
Itself, by itself solely, ONE everlastingly, and single.

— PLATO — *Sympos.*

With a feeling of deep yet most singular affection I regarded my friend Morella. Thrown by accident into her society many years ago, my soul, from our first meeting,
burned with fires it had never before known; but the fires
were not of Eros, and bitter and tormenting to my spirit
was the gradual conviction that I could in no manner de-
fine their unusual meaning, or regulate their vague intensity. Yet we met; and fate bound us together at the altar; and
I never spoke of passion, nor thought of love. She, however,
shunned society, and, attaching herself to me alone, rendered me happy. It is a happiness to wonder; — it is a happiness to dream.

Morella's erudition was profound. As I hope to live, her
talents were of no common order — her powers of mind
were gigantic. I felt this, and, in many matters, became her
pupil. I soon, however, found that, perhaps on account of
her Pressburg education, she placed before me a number of
those mystical writings which are usually considered the
mere dross of the early German literature. These, for what
reason I could not imagine, were her favorite and constant
study — and that, in process of time they became my own,
should be attributed to the simple but effectual influence of
habit and example.

In all this, if I err not, my reason had little to do. My convictions, or I forget myself, were in no manner acted upon by the ideal, nor was any tincture of the mysticism which I read, to be discovered, unless I am greatly mistaken, either in my deeds or in my thoughts. Persuaded of this, I abandoned myself implicitly to the guidance of my wife, and entered with an unflinching heart into the intricacies of her studies. And then — then, when, poring over forbidden pages, I felt a forbidden spirit enkindling within me — would Morella place her cold hand upon my own, and rake up from the ashes of a dead philosophy some low, singular words, whose strange meaning burned themselves in upon my memory. And then, hour after hour would I linger by her side, and dwell upon the music of her voice — until, at length, its melody was tainted with terror, — and there fell a shadow upon my soul — and I grew pale, and shuddered inwardly at those too unearthly tones. And thus, joy suddenly faded into horror, and the most beautiful became the most hideous, as Hinnôm became Gehenna.

It is unnecessary to state the exact character of those disquisitions which, growing out of the volumes I have mentioned, formed, for so long a time, almost the sole conversation of Morella and myself. By the learned in what might be termed theological morality they will be readily conceived, and by the unlearned they would, at all events, be little understood. The wild Pantheism of Fichte; the modified Παλιγγενεσια of Pythagoreans; and, above all, the doctrines of *Identity* as urged by Schelling, were generally the points of discussion presenting the most of beauty to the imaginative Morella. That identity which is termed personal, Mr. Locke, I think, truly defines to consist in the saneness of a rational being. And since by person we understand an intelligent essence having reason, and since there is a consciousness which always accompanies thinking, it is this which makes us all to be that which we call *ourselves* — thereby distinguishing us from other beings that think, and giving us our personal identity. But the *principium individuationis* — the notion of that identity *which at death is or is not lost for ever* — was to me, at all times, a consideration of intense interest; not more from the perplexing and exciting nature of its consequences, than from the marked and agitated manner in which Morella mentioned them.

But, indeed, the time had now arrived when the mystery of my wife's manner oppressed me as a spell. I could no longer bear the touch of her wan fingers, nor the low tone of her musical language, nor the lustre of her melancholy eyes. And she knew all this, but did not upbraid; she seemed conscious of my weakness or my folly, and, smiling, called it Fate. She seemed, also, conscious of a cause, to me unknown, for the gradual alienation of my regard; but she gave me no hint or token of its nature. Yet was she woman, and pined away daily. In time, the crimson spot settled steadily upon the cheek, and the blue veins upon the pale forehead became prominent; and, one instant, my nature melted into pity, but, in the next, I met the glance of her meaning eyes, and then my soul sickened and became giddy with the giddiness of one who gazes downward into some dreary and unfathomable abyss.

Shall I then say that I longed with an earnest and consuming desire for the moment of Morella's decease? I did; but the fragile spirit clung to its tenement of clay for many days — for many weeks and irksome months — until my tortured nerves obtained the mastery over my mind, and I grew furious through delay, and, with the heart of a fiend, cursed the days, and the hours, and the bitter moments, which seemed to lengthen and lengthen as her gentle life declined — like shadows in the dying of the day.

But one autumnal evening, when the winds lay still in heaven, Morella called me to her bedside. There was a dim mist over all the earth, and a warm glow upon the waters, and, amid the rich October leaves of the forest, a rainbow from the firmament had surely fallen.

"It is a day of days," she said, as I approached; "a day of all days either to live or die. It is a fair day for the sons of earth and life — ah, more fair for the daughters of heaven and death!"

I kissed her forehead, and she continued:

"I am dying, yet shall I live."

"Morella!"

"The days have never been when thou couldst love me — but her whom in life thou didst abhor, in death thou shalt adore."

"Morella!"

"I repeat that I am dying. But within me is a pledge of that affection — ah, how little! — which thou didst feel for me, Morella. And when my spirit departs shall the child live — thy child and mine, Morella's. But thy days shall be days of sorrow — that sorrow which is the most lasting of impressions, as the cypress is the most enduring of trees. For the hours of thy happiness are over; and joy is not gathered twice in a life, as the roses of Pæstum twice in a year. Thou shalt no longer, then, play the Teian with time, but, being ignorant of the myrtle and the vine, thou shalt bear about with thee thy shroud on the earth, as do the Moslemin at Mecca."

"Morella!" I cried, "Morella! how knowest thou this?" —

but she turned away her face upon the pillow, and, a slight tremor coming over her limbs, she thus died, and I heard her voice no more.

Yet, as she had foretold, her child — to which in dying she had given birth, which breathed not until the mother breathed no more — her child, a daughter, lived. And she grew strangely in stature and intellect, and was the perfect resemblance of her who had departed, and I loved her with a love more fervent than I had believed it possible to feel for any denizen of earth.

But, erelong, the heaven of this pure affection became darkened, and gloom, and horror, and grief, swept over it in clouds. I said the child grew strangely in stature and intelligence. Strange, indeed, was her rapid increase in bodily size — but terrible, oh! terrible were the tumultuous thoughts which crowded upon me while watching the development of her mental being! Could it be otherwise, when I daily discovered in the conceptions of the child the adult powers and faculties of the woman? — when the lessons of experience fell from the lips of infancy? and when the wisdom or the passions of maturity I found hourly gleaming from its full and speculative eye? When, I say, all this became evident to my appalled senses — when I could no longer hide it from my soul, nor throw it off from those perceptions which trembled to receive it — is it to be wondered at that suspicions, of a nature fearful and exciting, crept in upon my spirit, or that my thoughts fell back aghast upon the wild tales and thrilling theories of the entombed Morella? I snatched from the scrutiny of the world a being whom destiny compelled me to adore, and in the rigorous seclusion of my home, watched with an agonizing anxiety over all which concerned the beloved.

And, as years rolled away, and I gazed, day after day, upon her holy, and mild, and eloquent face, and poured over her maturing form, day after day did I discover new points of resemblance in the child to her mother, the melancholy and the dead. And, hourly, grew darker these shadows of similitude, and more full, and more definite, and more perplexing, and more hideously terrible in their aspect. For that her smile was like her mother's I could bear; but then I shuddered at its too perfect *identity* — that her eyes were like Morella's I could endure; but then they too often looked down into the depths of my soul with Morella's own intense and bewildering meaning. And in the contour of the high forehead, and in the ringlets of the silken hair, and in the wan fingers which buried themselves therein, and in the sad musical tones of her speech, and above all — oh! above all — in the phrases and expressions of the dead on the lips of the loved and the living, I found food for consuming thought and horror — for a worm that *would* not die.

Thus passed away two lustra of her life, and, as yet, my daughter remained nameless upon the earth. "My child," and "my love," were the designations usually prompted by a father's affection, and the rigid seclusion of her days precluded all other intercourse. Morella's name died with her at her death. Of the mother I had never spoken to the daughter; — it was impossible to speak. Indeed, during the brief period of her existence, the latter had received no impressions from the outer world, save such as might have been afforded by the narrow limits of her privacy. But at length the ceremony of baptism presented to my mind, in its unnerved and agitated condition, a present deliverance from the terrors of my destiny. And at the baptismal font I

hesitated for a name. And many titles of the wise and beautiful, of old and modern times, of my own and foreign
lands, came thronging to my lips, with many, many fair titles of the gentle, and the happy, and the good. What
prompted me, then, to disturb the memory of the buried
dead? What demon urged me to breathe that sound, which,
in its very recollection, was wont to make ebb the purple
blood in torrents from the temples to the heart? What fiend
spoke from the recesses of my soul, when, amid those dim
aisles, and in the silence of the night, I whispered within the
ears of the holy man the syllables — Morella? What more
than fiend convulsed the features of my child, and overspread them with hues of death, as starting at that scarcely
audible sound, she turned her glassy eyes from the earth to
heaven, and, falling prostrate on the black slabs of our an-
cestral vault, responded — "I am here!"

Distinct, coldly, calmly distinct, fell those few simple
sounds within my ear, and thence like molten lead, rolled
hissingly into my brain. Years — years may pass away, but
the memory of that epoch — never! Nor was I indeed ignorant of the flowers and the vine — but the hemlock and
the cypress overshadowed me night and day. And I kept no
reckoning of time or place, and the stars of my fate faded
from heaven, and therefore the earth grew dark, and its fig-
ures passed by me, like flitting shadows, and among them
all I beheld only — Morella. The winds of the firmament
breathed but one sound within my ears, and the ripples
upon the sea murmured evermore — Morella. But she
died; and with my own hands I bore her to the tomb; and
I laughed with a long and bitter laugh as I found no
traces of the first, in the charnel where I laid the second,
Morella.

SHADOW — A PARABLE

> Yea! though I walk through the valley of the *Shadow.*
> — *Psalm of David*

Ye who read are still among the living; but I who write shall have long since gone my way into the region of shadows. For indeed strange things shall happen, and secret things be known, and many centuries shall pass away, ere these memorials be seen of men. And, when seen, there will be some to disbelieve, and some to doubt, and yet a few who will find much to ponder upon in the characters here graven with a stylus of iron.

The year had been a year of terror, and of feelings more intense than terror for which there is no name upon the earth. For many prodigies and signs had taken place, and far and wide, over sea and land, the black wings of the Pestilence were spread abroad. To those, nevertheless, cunning in the stars, it was not unknown that the heavens wore an aspect of ill; and to me, the Greek Oinos, among others, it was evident that now had arrived the alternation of that seven hundred and ninety-fourth year when, at the entrance of Aries, the planet Jupiter is conjoined with the red ring of the terrible Saturnus. The peculiar spirit of the skies, if I mistake not greatly, made itself manifest, not only in the physical orb of the earth, but in the souls, imaginations, and meditations of mankind.

Over some flasks of the red Chian wine, within the walls

of a noble hall, in a dim city called Ptolemais, we say, at
night, a company of seven. And to our chamber there was
no entrance save by a lofty door of brass; and the door was
fashioned by the artisan Corinnos, and, being of rare work-
manship, was fastened from within. Black draperies, like-
wise, in the gloomy room, shut out from our view the
moon, the lurid stars, and the peopleless streets — but the
boding and the memory of Evil, they would not be so ex-
cluded. There were things around us and about of which
I can render no distinct account — things material and
spiritual — heaviness in the atmosphere — a sense of suf-
focation — anxiety — and, above all, that terrible state of
existence which the nervous experience when the senses are
keenly living and awake, and meanwhile the powers of
thought lie dormant. A dead weight hung upon us. It hung
upon our limbs — upon the household furniture — upon
the goblets from which we drank; and all things were depressed, and borne down thereby — all things save only the
flames of the seven iron lamps which illumined our revel.
Uprearing themselves in tall slender lines of light, they thus
remained burning all pallid and motionless; and in the mirror which their lustre formed upon the round table of
ebony at which we sat, each of us there assembled beheld
the pallor of his own countenance, and the unquiet glare in
the downcast eyes of his companions. Yet we laughed and
were merry in our proper way — which was hysterical;
and sang the songs of Anacreon — which are madness; and
drank deeply — although the purple wine reminded us of
blood. For there was yet another tenant of our chamber in
the person of young Zoilus. Dead, and at full length he lay,
enshrouded: — the genius and the demon of the scene.
Alas! he bore no portion in our mirth, save that his counte-

nance, distorted with the plague, and his eyes, in which
Death had but half extinguished the fire of the pestilence,
seemed to take such interest in our merriment as the dead
may haply take in the merriment of those who are to die.
But although I, Oinos, felt that the eyes of the departed
were upon me, still I forced myself not to perceive the bit-
terness of their expression, and, gazing down steadily into
the depths of the ebony mirror, sang with a loud and
sonorous voice the songs of the son of Teios. But gradually
my songs they ceased, and their echoes, rolling afar off
among the sable draperies of the chamber, became weak,
and undistinguishable, and so faded away. And lo! from
among those sable draperies where the sounds of the song
departed, there came forth a dark and undefined shadow —
a shadow such as the moon, when low in heaven, might
fashion from the figure of a man; but it was the shadow neither of man nor of God, nor of any familiar thing. And
quivering awhile among the draperies of the room, it at
length rested in full view upon the surface of the door of
brass. But the shadow was vague, and formless, and indefinite, and was the shadow neither of man nor God — neither God of Greece, nor God of Chaldæa, nor any Egyptian
God. And the shadow rested upon the brazen doorway, and
under the arch of the entablature of the door, and moved
not, nor spoke any word, but there became stationary and
remained. And the door whereupon the shadow rested was,
if I remember aright, over against the feet of the young
Zoilus enshrouded. But we, the seven there assembled,
having seen the shadow as it came out from among the
draperies, dared not steadily behold it, but cast down our
eyes, and gazed continually into the depths of the mirror of
ebony. And at length I, Oinos, speaking some low words,

THE SPHINX

During the dread reign of cholera in New York, I had accepted the invitation of a relative to spend a fortnight with him in the retirement of his *cottage ornée* on the banks of the Hudson. We had here around us all the ordinary means of summer amusement; and what with rambling in the woods, sketching, boating, fishing, bathing, music, and books, we should have passed the time pleasantly enough, but for the fearful intelligence which reached us every morning from the populous city. Not a day elapsed which did not bring us news of the decease of some acquaintance. Then, as the fatality increased, we learned to expect daily the loss of some friend. At length we trembled at the approach of every messenger. The very air from the South seemed to us redolent with death. That palsying thought, indeed, took entire possession of my soul. I could neither speak, think, nor dream of any thing else. My host was of a less excitable temperament, and, although greatly depressed in spirits, exerted himself to sustain my own. His richly philosophical intellect was not at any time affected by unrealities. To the substances of terror he was sufficiently alive, but of its shadows he had no apprehension.

His endeavors to arouse me from the condition of abnormal gloom into which I had fallen, were frustrated, in great measure, by certain volumes which I had found in his library. These were of a character to force into germination whatever seeds of hereditary superstition lay latent in my bosom. I had been reading these books without his knowledge, and thus he was then at a loss to account for the forcible impressions which had been made upon my fancy.

A favorite topic with me was the popular belief in omens — a belief which, at this one epoch of my life, I was almost seriously disposed to defend. On this subject we had long and animated discussions; he maintaining the utter groundlessness of faith in such matters, I contending that a popular sentiment arising with absolute spontaneity — that is to say, without apparent traces of suggestion — had in itself the unmistakable elements of truth, and was entitled to much respect.

The fact is, that soon after my arrival at the cottage there had occurred to myself an incident so entirely inexplicable, and which had in it so much of the portentous character, that I might well have been excused for regarding it as an omen. It appalled, and at the same time so confounded and bewildered me, that many days elapsed before I could make up my mind to communicate the circumstance to my friend.

Near the close of an exceedingly warm day, I was sitting, book in hand, at an open window, commanding, through a long vista of the river banks, a view of a distant hill, the face of which nearest my position had been denuded by what is termed a land-slide, of the principal portion of its trees. My thoughts had been long wandering from the volume before me to the gloom and desolation of the neighboring city.

Uplifting my eyes from the page, they fell upon the naked face of the hill, and upon an object — upon some living monster of hideous conformation, which very rapidly made its way from the summit to the bottom, disappearing finally in the dense forest below. As this creature first came in sight, I doubted my own sanity — or at least the evidence of my own eyes — and many minutes passed before I succeeded in convincing myself that I was neither mad nor in a dream. Yet when I describe the monster (which I distinctly saw, and calmly surveyed through the whole period of its progress), my readers, I fear, will feel more difficulty in being convinced of these points than even I did myself.

Estimating the size of the creature by comparison with the diameter of the large trees near which it passed — the few giants of the forest which had escaped the fury of the land-slide — I concluded it to be far larger than any ship of the line in existence. I say ship of the line, because the shape of the monster suggested the idea — the hull of one of our seventy-fours might convey a very tolerable conception of the general outline. The mouth of the animal was situated at the extremity of a proboscis some sixty or seventy feet in length, and about as thick as the body of an ordinary elephant. Near the root of this trunk was an immense quantity of black shaggy hair — more than could have been supplied by the coats of a score of buffaloes; and projecting from this hair downwardly and laterally, sprang two gleaming tusks not unlike those of the wild boar, but of infinitely greater dimension. Extending forward, parallel with the proboscis, and on each side of it, was a gigantic staff, thirty or forty feet in length, formed seemingly of pure crystal, and in shape a perfect prism — it reflected in the most gor-

geous manner the rays of the declining sun. The trunk was
fashioned like a wedge with the apex to the earth. From it
there were outspread two pairs of wings — each wing nearly
one hundred yards in length — one pair being placed above
the other, and all thickly covered with metal scales; each
scale apparently some ten or twelve feet in diameter. I observed that the upper and lower tiers of wings were con-
nected by a strong chain. But the chief peculiarity of this
horrible thing was the representation of a *Death's Head*,
which covered nearly the whole surface of its breast, and
which was as accurately traced in glaring white, upon the
dark ground of the body, as if it had been there carefully designed by an artist. While I regarded this terrific animal,
and more especially the appearance on its breast, with a
feeling of horror and awe — with a sentiment of forthcoming evil, which I found it impossible to quell by any effort
of the reason, I perceived the huge jaws at the extremity of
the proboscis suddenly expand themselves, and from them
there proceeded a sound so loud and so expressive of woe,
that it struck upon my nerves like a knell, and as the monster disappeared at the foot of the hill, I fell at once, faint-
ing, to the floor.

Upon recovering, my first impulse, of course, was to in-
form my friend of what I had seen and heard — and I can
scarcely explain what feeling of repugnance it was which, in
the end, operated to prevent me.

At length, one evening, some three or four days after the
occurrence, we were sitting together in the room in which
I had seen the apparition — I occupying the same seat at
the same window, and he lounging on a sofa near at hand.
The association of the place and time impelled me to give

him an account of the phenomenon. He heard me to the
end — at first laughed heartily — and then lapsed into an
excessively grave demeanor, as if my insanity was a thing beyond suspicion. At this instant I again had a distinct view
of the monster — to which, with a shout of absolute terror,
I now directed his attention. He looked eagerly — but
maintained that he saw nothing — although I designated
minutely the course of the creature, as it made its way down
the naked face of the hill.

I was now immeasurably alarmed, for I considered the
vision either as an omen of my death, or, worse, as the fore-
runner of an attack of mania. I threw myself passionately
back in my chair, and for some moments buried my face in
my hands. When I uncovered my eyes, the apparition was
no longer visible.

My host, however, had in some degree resumed the calmness of his demeanor, and questioned me very rigorously in
respect to the conformation of the visionary creature. When
I had fully satisfied him on this head, he sighed deeply, as if
relieved of some intolerable burden, and went on to talk,
with what I thought a cruel calmness, of various points of
speculative philosophy, which had heretofore formed subject of discussion between us. I remember his insisting very
especially (among other things) upon the idea that the principal source of error in all human investigations lay in the
liability of the understanding to underrate or to overvalue
the importance of an object, through mere misadmeasure-
ment of its propinquity. "To estimate properly, for example," he said, "the influence to be exercised on mankind at
large by the thorough diffusion of Democracy, the distance
of the epoch at which such diffusion may possibly be ac-

complished should not fail to form an item in the estimate.
Yet can you tell me one writer on the subject of government
who has ever thought this particular branch of the subject
worthy of discussion at all?"

He here paused for a moment, stepped to a book-case,
and brought forth one of the ordinary synopses of Natural
History. Requesting me then to exchange seats with him,
that he might the better distinguish the fine print of the
volume, he took my arm-chair at the window, and, opening
the book, resumed his discourse very much in the same
tone as before.

"But for your exceeding minuteness," he said, "in de-
scribing the monster, I might never have had it in my power
to demonstrate to you what it was. In the first place, let me
read to you a school-boy account of the genus *Sphinx*, of
the family *Crepuscularia*, of the order *Lepidoptera*, of the
class of *Insecta* — or insects. The account runs thus:

" 'Four membranous wings covered with little colored
scales of metallic appearance; mouth forming a rolled proboscis, produced by an elongation of the jaws, upon the
sides of which are found the rudiments of mandibles and
downy palpi; the inferior wings retained to the superior by
a stiff hair, antennæ in the form of an elongated club, pris-
matic; abdomen pointed. The Death's-headed Sphinx has
occasioned much terror among the vulgar, at times, by the
melancholy kind of cry which it utters, and the insignia of
death which it wears upon its corslet.' "

He here closed the book and leaned forward in the chair,
placing himself accurately in the position which I had occupied at the moment of beholding "the monster."

"Ah, here it is," he presently exclaimed — "it is reas-
cending the face of the hill, and a very remarkable looking

creature I admit it to be. Still, it is by no means so large or so distant as you imagined it; for the fact is that, as it wriggles its way up this thread, which some spider has wrought along the window-sash, I find it to be about the sixteenth of an inch in its extreme length, and also about the sixteenth of an inch distant from the pupil of my eye."